CU00408334

All in the Mind

By

Julia Pistrucci Malkin

Copyright © Julia Pistrucci Malkin 2018. All
rights reserved.

This book is dedicated to my husband Colin and my friend Jo. Without their help this book would never have existed.

Preface

This story is fictional, but the issues contained within it are real. Many people, including myself, have special needs issues. I have written this in the hope that readers can see the differences which these issues create on how they see themselves and their dealings with the world.

Julia Pistrucci Malkin, April 2018

Contents

Chapter One

The university buildings always reminded travellers of a bygone era. Architecture from the 1960s, tall grey buildings which looked more like factories rather than seats of learning, interspersed with pavement areas which at that time of year seemed so bare and colourless. It was late winter, and the occasional leafless tree added to the feeling of starkness and dullness. Life was only found in the groups of students, now in their second semester of their learning, and many recovering from the typical seasonal colds and influenza.

Dinesh was no exception. He had only just returned back from a trip to India to see his extended family when the flu hit him hard, the day in question being his first day back to his scientific studies. Clad constantly in a white lab coat, he was now telling a group of students in their lunch break about an experiment which had begun in his absence – an experiment which involved a collaboration of university departments, lecturers and students, which all were hoping had the possibility to change the lives of many.

The students he was chatting to were all first-years, one being the actual subject of the experiment. One student had to be chosen to endure a challenge – a challenge which had never been attempted before, but thanks to some psychological and technological advances, it had now become possible. The engineering department had pulled out all the stops; the best brains and minds had been engaged on the project, and success would mean great prestige and esteem for the standing of the university. Funding was secured, everything set up and running while Dinesh was away with influenza, and by the time he got back the whole of the Department of Engineering had been completely revamped. All that was missing was the subject for this experiment, a person who could withstand such a test of body and mind which had never ever been attempted before anywhere. Dinesh was assigned the task of finding this subject. Adam was tall, strong, excellent at sports, playing for the university football team in goal; he was the ideal candidate to withstand heavy physical and psychological pressure. This, coupled with a positive mental attitude, a busy social life and plenty of self-confidence, led Dinesh to offer him for the panel for selection.

He was proud and pleased when Adam was accepted.

With Adam was Brad, the captain of the football team, who was, as usual, ragging him about his constant lateness and laxity when it came to doing university work.

'I bet you haven't finished that essay yet, have you Adam! It's due in tomorrow!'

Adam turned round in a casual way to face his friend, the expression on his face revealing everything else except anxiety about his essay. 'Too busy,' was his response.

Brad continued to goad him. 'All you do is booze all night and play footy all day, don't you, Adam!' This time there was no verbal reaction, just a wry smile – Adam could never react in anger, no matter how much he was provoked.

Dinesh was more serious. 'I've never known anyone be late for assignment deadlines so much. Is he always like this?'

Amy, a student on the same module as Adam, stepped in when Adam didn't reply. 'You be thankful you're not doing his course. If it wasn't for me, he'd get nothing done at all.'

Adam's concentration, as always, was elsewhere. 'You know there's a big match soon. And you also know how important it is for us to win to stay on top of the table!'

'But the team practice session isn't till tomorrow,' Amy insisted. 'Why did you have to go for training last night? You could have that essay finished by now if you hadn't gone.'

'That was just me yesterday working with the new defender. I had to put him through his paces after Tim backed out.'

'He didn't back out,' Brad insisted. 'He was injured.'

'That's called backing out where I come from,' replied Adam. 'It would take more than a little sprain before they'd ever need to replace me!'

Another student came up, a worried look on his pale face. 'Adam? Dr Hewitt says you're to go up to his office right now. I don't know, but it might be something to do with your essays again.'

'Come on James! It's break! Tell him I'll be up in ten minutes.'

'OK,' James replied. He turned to leave, then looked back again at Adam. 'But you'll know how he'll react. He'll want you there now, you know how angry he gets.'

Adam just grinned; after all he could see nothing to worry about. There was another half an hour left to the end of break and if he was ten minutes late getting up to the office then that would still leave him spare time before the preparation for the experiment that afternoon. He stood lazily around, making no effort whatsoever to follow James to the office. However, Dinesh was upset – this was happening much too often.

'Ten minutes. You ought to have told him twenty.'

At this, both Brad and Adam burst out laughing. At this, Amy intervened.

'It's not funny. It really isn't! You're always late, Adam! Don't get into trouble again!'

Adam sighed and picked up his rucksack. 'Ok, I'm going.' He swung his rucksack over his shoulder. 'Be here when I get back. Won't be long.'

Brad just shrugged but Dinesh and Amy exchanged glances. Both of them had the feeling that Adam would be gone for longer than he thought...

Chapter Two

Adam arrived outside Dr Hewitt's office a full fifteen minutes after James asked him to attend. He'd made his way lazily to the building by way of a detour past the cafe, grabbed some crisps, stood around the lift eating them, and crammed himself into the lift with many others when it arrived. Once on the office floor, he'd hung around the door listening to a very angry Dr Hewitt, who seemed from outside the room to be ranting over the phone. For several minutes Adam delayed entering, knowing his lecturer's bad temper; but because the phone call didn't seem to show any signs of ending, he waited for a pause and knocked the door.

'It's this weekend, Atkins. Yes, this one coming! Honestly, don't they have diaries where you come from? For God's sake!' was the reply to Adam's knock. This was followed by a very loud 'Come in!!' directed towards the door.

Adam gently pushed the door open a fraction, till it was ajar; he went no further, because that angry voice had started again.

'Never mind the cold. What are you on about, coming down with a cold? You make sure it clears up before this weekend. Never mind the sneezing. Take something for it! First you haven't any way of keeping track of the date, and then you haven't got any cold pills. Where do you live, in a tent? Give me strength!!' This was followed by another shout at the door – 'COME IN!'

This time Adam entered, and now stood silently before the desk.

'Won't be a minute,' Hewitt said to Adam, before turning back to raging down the phone. 'Now, no excuses, Atkins. I want you down there. No, I do not care. You will not let me down. Or anyone else for that matter. No excuses. Do you hear me – No excuses!' He slammed down the receiver, shook his head, sighed and looked up at Adam.

Hewitt was tall and had a fierce demeanour, which gave him a look of great power even when sitting behind a desk in an office. He had black hair, a face white with anger, and sharp blue eyes which at that moment were burning straight into Adam.

'Sorry to bother you, but you sent for me,' said Adam, finding the confidence to look into his lecturer's angry face.

'That's true, I did send for you, but that phone call distracted me,' Hewitt replied. 'Sorry about that.' His temper began to rise once more as he remembered the call. 'All this work I've been putting in, preparing for an event this weekend and someone's calling me saying he's coming down with a cold! Have you ever known such lack of commitment? He'll be ringing up telling me he's in bed with that cold next! Anyway,' he paused for a few seconds to bring his temper back under control, 'that's all beside the point. I have called you because I want to talk about your essay. I assume, I suppose, that you know when it's due?'

'Tomorrow.'

'Do you also know that unless this one is handed in on time, there's a risk of your failing the module this year?'

Adam's usually confident face fell. 'No?'

'Well, surely by now someone must have warned you. Your personal tutor, she would have said something. I told her to. You know...what's her name...'

'Helen.'

Hewitt backed off a little. He'd never got used to the idea of students calling their lecturers by their first names. He had always insisted on a surname approach ever since he had arrived at the university. Students had hated his approach, and staff had opposed it, but he had held to that principle for many years; there were so many arguments about it that now it had reached the point where nobody would dare oppose it. And that was what he liked and what he was used to now – respect without any opposition.

This is why he had never got on well with Adam. His constant lax attitude towards the work had often aroused the worst in Hewitt's anger and it had got to the extent where Adam would want to be anywhere else in the uni other than Hewitt's office. Even cleaning the toilets was preferable to Adam than having to stand in that same small room, facing that same angry face which he knew every single line of after being summoned to the office so regularly over his four months of study.

Hewitt paused. 'Helen? Helen Connors, you mean? Yes. That's her. Surely she's warned you?'

Adam tried to act casual, hoping to prevent a full lecture. 'She may have done.'

But Hewitt started on him again. 'You're not only handing everything in late but the standard of your work needs to be improved. Now you're an intelligent guy. You're talented. I don't want you missing out. I don't know whether you know, but...'

Adam let his eyes slowly wander round the room while his lecturer was grilling him. His mind wandered to the experiment later that afternoon. He was confident about it. The whole lot was a sham and he knew it. Nothing would happen to him. He had been briefed on what could happen, and he was going in there deliberately to prove everyone wrong. He'd be totally unchanged. Afterwards, he'd be having his name plastered all over the university, on their websites, in the press; everyone would be speaking his name, showing his picture, all praising him for going through such an arduous test...thoughts came into his mind of standing in front of applauding crowds of students and lecturers as he was presented with awards...by that time he wasn't listening to Hewitt at all and his eyes wandered further round the room – and they came to eventually rest on a strange object which looked completely out of place in the office of a university lecturer.

It was sleek, smooth and shining black, sitting on a corner of Hewitt's desk. It was a helmet - a fully enclosed helmet, not just headwear for the top of the head, or a mask for the face, but a full helmet. It was one which enclosed the whole head, the sort which made it appear as if the wearer could neither breathe properly nor see well with it on. No part of the head or face would be visible or exposed when it was worn.

Adam did not recognise it as being the helmet of a film character, or anything from history. In fact he didn't know what it represented at all. Yet there it was, in front of him on his lecturer's desk.

It looked so out of place in that office, alongside the computer and telephone, the pens and papers, the books and files, that Adam broke out immediately into a grin which turned into an automatic laugh.

It was a small laugh, but nonetheless a laugh which Hewitt overheard even when lecturing at full throttle. It cut him mid-sentence.

'And furthermore, when you enter your next year, and find that your grades are...Adam! What was that? On top of all this, you're now taking every single word I'm saying as nothing but one big joke!'

Adam stopped, the grin leaving his face at once. 'I'm sorry,' he began, 'It's not a joke. Not at all. That's not what I was laughing at, of course it wasn't. It was this.' He strolled over towards the desk, his cheeky grin returning as he focused on the helmet again. 'I was laughing at this! What on earth is this crazy thing doing in here?' He went over and picked it up. 'Nice toy, is it for your kids?'

To Adam's surprise, Hewitt started up; he rose from the desk at speed, walked round to Adam and snatched the helmet away from him, straight out of his hands. 'No!' he snapped at once. 'As a matter of fact, that happens to be mine!' He then placed it, with great care, on a shelf behind his desk and therefore well out of Adam's reach, while Adam simply stared incredulously, wondering what was so precious about a children's toy.

Hewitt turned and saw Adam's gaping mouth. He changed the subject at once to prevent further questioning. 'About that essay. It's important it's all done by tomorrow. Do you hear me? Important.' Adam felt those sharp blue eyes burn into him once again.

'Alright. Important.'

'And you remember how to present it?'

'Two files, one emailed to you and one to Helen.' Hewitt cringed again at the sound of the name. 'And two hard copies which need to be given to the undergraduate office.'

'By what time?'

'Midday.'

'Good. You can go.' Hewitt turned away and Adam, a very relieved look on his face, at last exited that office to return to lunch.

Chapter Three

Outside the doors to the Department of Engineering, an anxious Dinesh stood waiting for Adam to return. He was outlining the nature of that experiment he was so proud to take part in, trying to explain it to Brad and Amy so they'd know what – and who – to expect later that afternoon.

'You mean Adam will be a different person?' Amy asked with worry etched all over her face.

'Yes, if all goes well,' Dinesh replied. 'Everything has been specially designed to create a person with traits of special support needs – things like traits of dyspraxia, Asperger syndrome, maybe even a phobia or something like that. It all depends on the person. Now, because of the dramatic differences between one person and another, it is impossible to say just what differences Adam will have. There could be changes in personality, temperament, social abilities, relating to people, and communication skills. His hobbies and interests could change. There could be geekiness or eccentricity. There could be anxiety or depression. Abilities could appear in different fields, and with other skills he could need more support.'

'Will all of this be permanent?' Amy was looking more alarmed by the minute.

'No. Only for a week,' Dinesh replied. 'A week will be enough for changes to be seen, support needs noted, and then one more session in our special machine and I can guarantee that Adam will be back to his old self!'

'But, what's the point of doing all this to Adam?'

'Amy, don't worry, Adam will be fine, and he's doing it to help others. Special educational needs people will need support at university, then there's people with depression – think of how many people this university could help! There's many different conditions affecting people, and each one is different which is why we are trying to generate different conditions in one individual. Now, that's the big key to the experiment – only by seeing everything through the eyes of a person with these conditions can we understand the type of support they need.'

'But surely they're all the same?' Brad asked disbelievingly.

16

'No, they are not, no way are they the same,' Dinesh replied emphatically. 'Are we all the same as people? No, we aren't, and Asperger people aren't all alike either. Some are solitary while others have a few friends. Dyspraxic people are different too, because some just have difficulties in some areas while in others it's affecting them in most areas of their lives. Dyspraxia can affect memory, or throwing and catching a ball, for example. There's no such thing as a one-size-fits-all when it comes to university support. But many of these people are clever – they just need support with their learning and studies. Imagine the potential these people have at universities, if the departments all knew the support that they needed, and could provide that support!'

'How many people could benefit from this?' asked Amy.

'Well, different studies disagree as to how many special needs people there are, but some statistics put the figure at one in five if mental health issues are included. That's twenty per cent of the population.'

'Well I think it's crazy,' Brad stated defiantly. 'Are you seriously telling me that this money is just to help twenty per cent? What about the other eighty? And what makes this twenty per cent so special that they deserve it in the first place? We're all the same and should be treated the same. Nobody should get special treatment. No matter whom they are!'

Brad swung his rucksack over his shoulder and made to leave just as Adam was returning.

'Brad, what's up? You OK?'

'Ask Dinesh and his bloody department. They certainly know how to spend money. Give it to twenty per cent and let the rest go without.' He didn't wait for a reply but headed off towards the lecture halls.

'What's going on?'

'It's OK, Adam. Brad didn't understand the importance of the work we're doing,' Dinesh replied. 'But hopefully he will, when the experiment gets under way. Come on, it's nearly time for the briefing.'

'Great!' grinned Adam. 'And then you'll all be later on admiring my wonderful new brain!'

'We aren't doing anything like that...'

'It's a joke. Just a joke, lighten up! But seriously, I know who definitely needs a new brain right now. That's old Hewitt. Guess what I've just seen in his office just now. I couldn't believe it when I saw it. Go on, guess!'

Amy and Dinesh paused.

'A beer can?'

'Amy!' Adam laughed. 'You know old Hewitt wouldn't allow one of those in there. Do you remember when I...'

'Yes I do,' Amy replied, hastily. 'And I don't want to remember it again, thank you very much.'

'Well, go on guessing!'

'Honestly, I can't think of anything. So, what was in his office?'

Adam started laughing. 'You'll never believe this – it was a strange black helmet!'

'You mean – like Vikings or something?'

'It looked strange. Funny thing, it was. I couldn't believe it. But guess what happened next! There I was, just holding it – and old Hewitt just snatched it out my hand as if I was contaminating it! Now that's crazy. If there's any brains wanting working on, his should be first.'

'Right, let's get you down there now for briefing,' Dinesh interrupted as Brad burst out laughing. 'Can you come, Amy?'

'No I can't, I've a lecture now,' she replied sadly. 'It's a pity. I'd have loved to have seen this!'

Adam grinned. 'There'll be nothing to see.'

'What do you mean?'

'I know that machine won't do a thing to me. Here am I, supposedly getting traits of all this and change into someone else. But it's all fake. It's not real. All this special needs stuff. Do you really think someone could be like that? Seriously? It's just someone somewhere sitting in an office making all this up. Probably with the government or the university paying them a fortune to discover it. And I'm going to prove it. That's why I'm doing it – to prove there is no such thing as Aspergers, or dyspraxia, things like this aren't real.'

'How many times have I been through all this?' Dinesh began. But his words fell on deaf ears. Adam just grinned back and pointed to his head.

'It's all in the mind!'

Chapter Four

The Department of Engineering was looking very much like something out of a sci-fi movie. Three of the main rooms had been completely renovated – all the standard university tools and equipment had been moved out and sophisticated electronic equipment had been brought in especially for the experimental week. Some pieces had been made solely for the purpose of this experiment, and had taken years to design and produce, while other items had been hired or drafted in for the purpose.

Dinesh and Adam walked through a large room full of hastily stacked tables, stools and engineering hand tools and through a side door into the main experimental area. This was dominated by a huge glass chamber, large enough for a person to lie down in. It was rounded like a cylindrical tube and split into two halves lengthways, like a large commercial sunbed. The area where the head would be was surrounded by wiring, computer equipment, monitors, video machines and various other electronic technologies. Along one of the walls were control panels and screens. Several white-coated technicians were running final equipment checks, calling out letter and number codes and replying 'Check' after each one. All this reminded Adam of a TV programme about the control area for the lunar landings of the late 1960s.

Supervising the experiment was the head of the Department of Psychology, Professor Elizabeth Mason, a blonde woman who gave them a smile as Adam and Dinesh walked in. She looked very calm, neat and well turned out in comparison to her associate, Dr Edward Young, a tall, black man with a soiled lab coat, the pockets of which were bulging with hand tools and wires. He was one of the senior lecturers in the Department of Engineering and was constantly on the move adjusting monitors and controls. He had been very stressed about this experiment taking over three whole main rooms of his department and was also very concerned about how this new equipment would respond when linked to the university's main computers. In the background were electronic engineering students being guided through the checks the technicians were making. The sound of voices and bleeping monitors permeated the room.

'Hi Adam!' Professor Mason sounded as cheerful as ever. 'Dinesh, could you do me a favour and initiate start up on monitor 5?'

'Sure.' He went to help Dr Young on the other side of the room as Professor Mason approached.

'Now Adam,' she began, 'I'm Professor Mason, but you can call me Liz if you're nice. And that's Dr Young. Just call him Ed. Let's show you round. Ed! Come over when you're done and show Adam round the chamber area.'

'Hi Ed!'

'Fine medical report!' Ed called across to him. 'Everything checked out!'

'I'd expect nothing less,' was the confident reply.

'Any coughs or sneezes since? Feeling well?'

'I'm fine.'

'Good. You'll be amazed how much a cough or sneeze will affect our equipment here. I've been spending weeks adjusting all this. One sneeze and you're out of here!'

'OK,' grinned Adam as Ed approached him.

Ed took Adam to the chamber. 'Here's where you'll be. Comfy, eh? There'll be plenty going on around you – and even inside you – but don't worry, you'll be out cold when we do this. We're waiting on Dr Keller to turn up. He's the medical mastermind, and nobody in here's going to dream about running this thing without him in the room! Rest assured, we've the best brains and the best kit from three departments. Engineering wizards, psychology experts and the medical guys. All in on what's a first of its kind!'

'What about us?' came an indignant voice from what seemed to be a small ante-room off the main room. A bald, bespectacled head stuck out from behind a door.

'Oh, yeah, not forgetting the amazing Dr Hollis from the Information Technology department.'

'Call me Joe. Come and see these wonderful machines, and meet some of the brains behind the business.'

Adam was led into a small room where computer units were stacked up from floor to ceiling, wall to wall, across two full walls, while three technicians sat at desk monitors on another wall. They looked up as Adam entered, wanting to see their subject they'd be testing at last. The room was very cold and Adam shivered.

'Chilly isn't it?' began Joe. 'We have to keep these units cool. The heat affects them; we need the air-con full on.'

'Adam?' called Liz. 'Dr Keller is here. Time for your first video session.'

Adam offered a cold hand to Dr Keller and sat down confidently at a monitor Liz had pointed out to him.

'Now Adam,' Liz said, putting a video recording unit and microphone in front of Adam, 'It's important to say exactly how you're feeling. These video logs will be taken as records of your progress. What you're feeling, what you're doing, everything is important no matter how silly or trivial it may seem to you. Take as long as you wish. Nothing will be ever edited out.'

Adam brought the microphone closer to him, waited for the signal – Liz loaded a file entitled, 'Video One – Tuesday' - and then began speaking...

'I'm here now...I'm in the lab. I'm just about to do something crazy, as always. I can't believe I'm doing this. I shall be in this chamber behind me for only a few minutes, so I'm told, but they are telling me I will be coming out as someone different. Somebody else. To me that's impossible but that's what they're telling me will happen. A person with traits of special support needs, like dyspraxia or Asperger syndrome...well, I don't even believe in it. Crazy.' He couldn't resist a grin and a small laugh, not even on a live camera. 'I don't really know what will happen, or how I will feel afterwards, but I'm sure Liz and Ed know what they're doing. And if all else fails there's a doctor right here so I think I'm safe enough. They're a good team, we will work well together because they've got the best brains for this job and I've got the best body for it!' he laughed again as Liz stood beside him. 'How's that?'

'Excellent,' Ed replied, turning off the mic. 'Couldn't be better.'

'OK,' Liz walked away, calling Adam and Dr Keller over to the chamber. 'It's time.'

'Right, Adam. What I want you to do is to get into here. Feet first, then one shot and you'll be totally out in a few minutes. No worries. Ready?'

Adam did as he was instructed, sitting on the edge of the glass chamber then turning to put his feet in position first, then laying down. While Liz and Dr Keller fitted the head apparatus and wiring up, Ed and Dinesh checked over the monitors with the technicians. Ed called for confirmation of signals being received in the computer room; Joe once again stuck his head out from behind the door and replied with a thumbs-up.

The wiring felt strange to Adam. He could hear the bleeping of the medical equipment being turned on – heart rate and blood pressure readings being watched carefully by Dr Keller. Then Liz was running checks on the monitors, making her way round the room calmly, in comparison to Ed who was racing around checking everyone and everything over and over again at high speed as if he was expecting anything to go wrong any minute.

'Ok Adam, time to say goodnight,' Dr Keller said, administering propofol. 'What I want you to do is count down from 100. Ready? 100...'

'99...98...97...96...' Adam couldn't say any more as blackness engulfed him.

After taking a final readings check, Liz closed the chamber and sealed it.

Dr Keller smiled. 'Ok guys,' he said, looking round at everyone. 'You have between five and ten minutes, sooner the better.'

'Right,' Ed began. 'Initiate program 1, follow on in 20 seconds with program 2, level 5, check progress monitors 6 and 7, frequencies 10 though 12...'

Everyone calmly followed orders.

Chapter Five

It was dark. Pitch dark. Adam awoke suddenly, conscious of nothing but darkness. Then feeling sweat on his face. Soon, blurred shapes slowly began appearing around him. Then a kind of hazy light surrounded him completely.

'Adam?'

Who said that...who called him by name? He began to panic a little, as all he could see were blurred heads looking over him.

'Adam, this is Dr Keller. Can you hear me?'

Adam tried to speak but could not. All he could manage was a slight nod of the head.

'Check monitor 6!'

'It's OK,' Dinesh called back. 'It all checks out, he's coming round.'

'Bring some water right now. He may need a rehydration mix made up.' One of the technicians left the room.

Adam could first see three heads clearing above him, and then he could slowly make out three faces – Liz, Ed and Dr Keller. He was confused – he could remember the names but for some reason the faces seemed far more obscure than they were prior. What had changed about these people?

'Liz?'

'Glad to have you back with us, Adam.'

'Back with you?'

'Yes,' Liz replied. 'You've been out for seven minutes. Don't you remember?'

Very faded images of monitor screens and having an injection came into his mind, but he couldn't remember how long ago all this took place.

'I'm sweating,' was the only reply he could manage as he pulled himself slowly out of the chamber.

'Dinesh! Check on level 8 section 7.'

'Hydration falling.'

'Where's that water?'

Dr Keller took the cup from the technician and then began the hydration mix. 'You'll feel better in a few minutes.'

Adam just stared round, totally amazed by the sounds, lights, colours, actions, people...

'Adam?'

No response.

'Adam!'

He turned towards Dr Keller with a rather confused expression.

'Drink this.'

Adam slowly drank the hydration mix. Liz, Ed and Dinesh were monitoring the readouts.

'Dinesh, get hold of Amy and tell her to come here. She was worried about Adam so it would help if she saw he was OK.'

As Dinesh left, Joe strode in confidently from the computer room.

'Ed! Our machines could take the strain, what do you think of that!'

'Ok. Please don't say, I told you so.'

'How's the patient?'

Adam didn't respond. Dr Keller turned. 'He's just finishing the rehydration mix. Then we'll take some readings and run some checks.'

Liz came over. 'All monitors check out, we need to run the coordination checks now. Adam, you OK?'

'Yes, thanks, just finished this.' He gave the cup back to Dr Keller as Liz began removing the wires and head apparatus.

'OK Adam. Thumb to finger.'

The only response Liz got was a blank look, then after a pause of several seconds, a hesitant question. 'Which thumb to which finger?'

'Left hand first, left thumb to index finger, that's it. Now the next finger, that's it, just like we practised. Don't you remember?'

'How was I supposed to know which one? You didn't tell me!'

Liz and Ed exchanged glances.

'You're doing fine,' Liz reassured Adam. 'Left hand first, then the right.'

Adam continued the checks. Hands were done first, and then eyes were checked to see if they were able to follow movements. Tests were done to check for dizziness and all medical monitors given another readout check before the remainder of the wiring was removed.

Amy then arrived with Dinesh. Adam was sitting on the outside of the chamber, with Liz, Ed, Joe and Dr Keller in close attendance.

'You feel OK?' Amy asked as she walked up to them. She was smiling at Adam, and then looked at Ed for reassurance, who smiled back.

Adam didn't reply. He could see Amy was looking at him first, but then she was looking at Ed. He'd realised – how did he know that it was him she was talking to? He didn't! She had looked at him but she'd looked at Ed too! Something deep inside was warning him – a fear, something deep, that it was wrong to make a mistake. So he did not reply. He daren't, in case Amy was asking someone else.

'Adam! Are you alright?'

This time Adam knew Amy was talking to him so he answered at once. 'A bit sweaty. Were you talking to me before?'

'Yes. I was.'

'Then I'm sorry I didn't answer but you were looking at Ed when you asked the question. I didn't know you were talking to me.'

Amy was amazed at the frustrated and upset look on Adam's face.

'Amy, it's because I was in a group. There's Liz, and Joe with me from the computer room and Ed from engineering and...'

'You don't need to explain. It's OK.' She turned to Liz with a very worried look. 'Is everything alright?'

'Couldn't be better,' Liz replied. 'Please try not to worry. This social difficulty is one of the traits of the special support needs which the experiment has produced in you. There could be others occurring over the course of the experiment.' Then she addressed the whole team. 'If there's anything you see over the next few days which could relate to this experiment, please let me know, no matter how slight or trivial, it all needs to be recorded.'

'What's going to happen next?'

'Adam's staying here for half an hour just in case there are any problems. We're going to have the med checks made and after that he's free to leave.'

Amy's face looked even more worried than before.

Chapter Six

Liz had checked everything out with Adam. Apart from the dehydration problem, which the sachet mix which Dr Keller had given him had sorted out, there were no physical problems. Psychologically, there were elements of confusion and perception errors which were coupled with increased sensory sensitivity.

'Now, at present we are not sure whether or not these problems are caused by the response to the experimental procedure or if they're actual traits of special support needs being produced,' Liz told the others, watching Adam. He was standing perfectly still to study the lights on the monitoring equipment. 'Dinesh, what we'll do now is to go through another video log and then if you could take him down to the cafe for break that would be perfect.'

'So technically I'm in charge of him when we leave the lab?' Dinesh said with a smile, looking forward to the responsibility.

'While he's on the uni campus you're assigned to look after him,' Ed replied. 'But remember, mind, if you see anything unusual or different in him there must be a record. I don't care how you do it, Photos, written logs, I don't care if it's yellow post-it notes for God's sake. You keep that record.'

Dinesh felt proud. Now he wasn't just a science student – he was an important part of one of the greatest scientific experiments ever done at his university.

'We're assigning him to you because you've known Adam since school,' said Liz. 'You know him. You know everything about him - Adam the student, Adam the friend, Adam the man. You know him, his family, everything. To us he's an experimental candidate, but you've known him so long that you'll notice changes in him well before we do. Now, remember what Ed said. Anything, write it down. Even something you think could be trivial, it doesn't matter how silly or how small it is. Keep a log.'

Dinesh agreed.

'Adam, time for your second video session,' Dr Keller intervened. He had finished all the med check test notes and was setting up the mic. Adam, still fascinated by the lights, didn't move.

What was it about the sequence which fascinated him? Was it the repeating, the change of colours? Adam was compelled to watch, to keep counting, no matter what happened, he had to keep trying to get it right...over again...over again...nothing else mattered, nothing did matter, he'd only become more frustrated if he couldn't get it right...he had to keep going...*I can get up to twenty*, he thought. *Must make it twenty-one. Must make it twenty-one...*

'Adam,' Liz said, managing at last to get him to move, and bringing him to the desk, 'Remember, just like the first time we did it. Say how you're feeling even if it sounds silly. Are you ready?'

Adam looked away back to the lights again and turned to Liz. He nodded as Liz loaded up a file entitled 'Video Two – Tuesday' and then signalled for him to start.'

'Well...' he began.

'Take your time.'

'Well, it's very difficult, very difficult. There are all these lights everywhere, on the equipment around me. I've never seen lights like these before. I'm trying to memorise the pattern sequences but I keep getting stuck at about the twentieth or so. Then it'sj frustrating having to wait till the sequence resumes and then I have to try all over again. It's so frustrating. In fact it's making me quite angry. I've never felt anything likc this before.'

Liz immediately left him and began typing into another computer at high speed. Ed followed.

'Liz is asking me how I feel all the time. That sounds so pointless, so silly. As if feelings count, as if they matter, but they don't. It's the facts I'm looking for. What's real, not what I feel. That doesn't mean a thing to me.' He was frowning, his voice speeding up on the recording. 'I can understand if it's about health of course, since if I'm in any pain I'll tell Dr Keller at once. But to ask me how I'm feeling? That's not the same as pain. Therefore there's no point to it,' he finished finally with a nod of the head.

Dinesh smiled.

Adam continued. 'So the only feeling I've got is anger. And that counts to me. There's a point to that and a reason for it – because every time I'm trying to configure the pattern of those monitor lights I can only go up to the twentieth,

40

when the one on the fifth column on the second machine turns red. Then I'm trying to anticipate which one the next one will be, I can't anticipate it at the moment. I want twenty-one, and I get frustrated by it and that's making me angry.' He looked round. Liz wasn't there beside him. 'Liz? Liz!'

'It's OK, I'm here,' she called back, walking hastily towards him from the computer. 'I'm still here, no need to worry.'

'I think that's all, I hope that's what you wanted,' Adam looked at Liz and Dinesh with a worried look.

Liz smiled back in her usual calm way. 'That will do fine.'

'Time for break, Adam,' Dinesh said confidently.

Adam's worried face stared back at him.

Chapter Seven

A university cafe is always a crowded place. Crowds round the tables, crowds collecting trays and crowds queuing up for the coffee. This break was no exception. Then there was the noise, the constant sound of laughter, chatter, clatter of cups, knives and forks.

Adam was totally lost in all the confusion of sound and vision by the time they arrived. Brad was already waiting at a table with Amy, but that didn't stop Adam feeling very uneasy with the whole experience. As he sat down with Dinesh and a coffee put in front of him, the bewilderment of the environment was beginning to affect his concentration.

'Adam, you OK?' Brad asked.

'That's strange.'

'What is?'

'I never noticed before just how noisy and crowded it is in here,' was Adam's nervous reply.

Brad burst out laughing – a strong, hearty, immediate loud laugh, much to the amazement of Adam, who clearly had no idea what he found so funny.

'What did I say?' he asked, turning to his friend.

Brad said nothing. Instead, he just carried on laughing. Adam's amazement turned quickly to annoyance.

'Brad – what did I say? Tell me!'

Brad ignored Adam completely, lost in laughter. Adam's annoyance was rapidly turning to anger. Amy saw it at once.

'Stop it, Brad!'

Brad looked at Adam and grinned. 'I always knew you were a head-case, Adam, but that takes it.'

The unfamiliar term added confusion to the anger. 'A...a head-case?'

Dinesh hurriedly interrupted, sensing what was coming. 'Adam, Brad just thought something was funny, that's all. But it's OK now. Everything's cool. Just relax.'

Adam slowly began to calm down as Dinesh gave Brad a warning look. Silence fell on the table. Dinesh took advantage of it and started a new conversation – he changed the subject quickly.

'Adam, when are you going to do Dr Hewitt's essay?'

Amy caught hold of the subject change, adding to the conversation in the hope that it would help Adam calm down. 'Mine's nearly done. It should be ready by tomorrow. It needs to be. Tomorrow's the deadline.'

But Brad seized another opportunity to intentionally annoy Adam. 'I've done mine,' he said with gloating confidence. Then in a more worried tone, he added, 'I bet Adam's not done his, though! He never does anything on time! I bet he's forgotten!'

There was a pause. Adam hated the fact that there he was, sitting at that table, and here was someone talking about him to everyone else using third-party language and not addressing him directly. Why was Brad talking to the others and not him? He stayed still for a few seconds, considering the best way to reply. This was difficult, as everyone on that table was looking at him. But he finally managed to string a few words together into a sentence. *Why is it so hard to find the right words?*

'No I haven't forgotten.' Adam was serious, polite, speaking directly at Brad with no signs of any emotion showing in his face. 'It'll be done on time. Don't worry.'

This was so funny to Brad that he burst into another fit of laughter. After all, hadn't Adam been late with every single assignment that year? Didn't he always turn up late to every lecture and every seminar? Wasn't he late that very morning, when Dr Hewitt wanted to see him in his office? And now he's now saying that this essay – which was due to be handed in the very next day – would be done on time! To Brad this was hilarious. It wasn't to Adam, however, who turned round to stare at him.

'What's the joke?'

Brad took no notice whatsoever.

'I asked you a question,' Adam asked, louder. 'What's the joke?'

Brad ignored him completely, he was just grinning back.

'What's the joke!'

Brad's face turned into a sneer. He pointed at Adam.

'I'll tell you what's the joke. You're the joke! You've never given an assignment in on time in your life! How many times has Dr Hewitt reminded you of the deadline? And everyone else has had to as well!'

Adam's anger increased in his face as Brad laughed again at him.

'And now you sit there telling me that you'll get an essay ready for him tomorrow! I bet you've done no work on it yet at all! That's the biggest joke I've heard this week! Who are you kidding? If it wasn't for Amy and me you'd have nothing done at all, and you know it. You know it!'

Adam's face was white with anger but he still responded with no emotion. 'I'll do it. If I say I will, I will.'

Adam got up to leave. Picking up his rucksack, he turned to the table to see Brad still laughing at him. Adam paused. *Why can't I find*

the right words at the right time when I need
them?

'I'm going to the library. Leave me
alone.'

Without waiting for a reply, Adam got up,
leaving an astonished audience behind. He
walked straight out of the cafe and turned
towards the library building. Brad just looked
amazed at seeing Adam leave. Amy looked
worried. But Dinesh was angry.

'I tried to warn you, Brad, but you didn't
stop, did you? You kept on and on, laughing at
him. But it's not funny! He's serious about that
essay. You've got to understand, he is. That's not
the sort of thing he'd joke about. He may have
done before, but not now. He's serious. If he says
that essay will be ready by the deadline
tomorrow, it will be.'

'What the hell's up with him?' Brad had
never seen Adam walk out on him.

'I've never known him go to the library in
his life!' said Amy.

Brad grinned again. 'It doesn't matter
now if he goes to the library or not,' he stated

confidently. 'I mean, here we are, late afternoon and a 2000-word assignment essay due tomorrow. And he hasn't done a thing, not a damn thing. But he sits on that chair and he tells me that it'll be done on time. Who the hell does he think he is - a genius? He hasn't got a hope of ever getting it done and he knows it. Now he says he's going to the library, but that's just to save his own lousy face. He'll end up in the pub as usual.'

'You must believe me, 'Dinesh argued, 'If he says he'll get that essay done on time, it will be.'

'No way,' retorted Brad. 'Tomorrow he'll be in trouble again. He will be, and I'm gonna just love it. You know how angry old Hewitt gets, and it's gonna be great. I'll be sitting there in that room, watching him get into trouble and I'll be smiling back at him as he's getting humiliated in front of everyone else. And that'll serve him right for being so cocky and walking out on me. Moron.'

'I can't see him getting it done either,' Amy was worried; 'Doesn't the library close in ten minutes? He hasn't got a chance!'

'Exactly,' smiled Brad. He lay back in his chair. After all, he was looking forward to the following day. It certainly was going to be fun.

Chapter Eight

Dinesh was in Liz's office. He'd been told to report later that day with his notes, knocked at the door, told to enter and was now waiting for the Head of the Department of Psychology to finish her phone call. He was checking through his notes. It was a responsible job, looking after Adam, being a part of this great experiment, but he was feeling rather apprehensive about it after what he'd witnessed in that cafe earlier that day. In fact, he was wondering if he'd bitten off more than he could chew by agreeing to take it on.

'Right, I'll see you in a few minutes. Dinesh is here now.' Liz put down the phone and turned to Dinesh. 'That was Ed. He'll be in as soon as he's supervised the engineer technicians in the lab.'

'OK,' Dinesh responded hesitantly.

'What's the problem?'

'Well,' Dinesh said with a sigh, 'I'm just wondering if I've done the right thing. With this experiment, I mean. You see, what happened in that cafe...'

'You've already told me once, it's fine, don't worry.'

'It's not just Adam I'm worried about though. It's Brad.'

'Because he was joking to Adam about his being late all the time?'

'Partly. But it's more than that. After Adam left, Brad then said he was looking forward to Adam getting into trouble with Dr Hewitt for not getting that essay done. Adam doesn't know that Brad's waiting to make trouble and to use Adam to get a huge laugh about that essay...'

'But you said Adam would be in the library? Getting it done on time?'

'Yes,' Dinesh replied, 'But how is Adam going to get it finished for tomorrow? There's a 99.99% chance he's never even started it till now. Even if he goes to the library and gets out the right books...'

Liz leaned forward. 'There's a high chance Adam has traits of Aspergers now, after that experiment. One of the traits of Aspergers that often comes through is tenacity – many of them, when they find a subject they get really passionate about, can pour their hearts and souls into it. Many of them get immersed into projects, they can learn about one subject in great detail. They get fascinated by details. And because of that, they can lose track of time. If I'm right, and Adam has traits of Aspergers in this regard, then once he's in that library it'll be hard to stop him.'

Dinesh stared back.

'You said he's in that library now?' Liz continued. 'I don't think he'll take those books out at all. He'll have them with him while he's on that essay – he'll be working on it actually in that library. The big key is don't interrupt him – any distractions and frustration will set in. I just hope everything will be all right in there.'

There was a knock at the door and Ed entered, his soiled coat looking more soiled than ever.

'Come in Ed, we've covered Dinesh's experiences with Adam and they're going to get copied up tonight. Now, I know you're not a psychologist, but...'

'I just program those machines,' Ed interrupted, sitting down heavily. 'I hope it all checks out in there after all this.'

'But we need everyone's feedback on this, including yours,' finished Liz. 'What were your observations today?'

'Well...we know Adam's in good health, he stood the process with no problems, Dr Keller fixed the dehydration...there's just a few emotional changes...'

'Such as?'

'Well, there's that video - especially that point where he's mentioning how he's being distracted by the lights. He seemed as if he was experiencing something he'd never felt before.'

'That's why I went straight off to type up, what you saw could be similar to what I could see.'

'What could you see?' Dinesh asked.

'Frustration, and a lot of it,' Liz replied. 'Several different sorts. First, the frustration at being distracted in the first place. Then that count Adam was doing, he was trying to count the lights, but it kept stopping. That was frustrating him too. Then that anger he told us about – that could be the result of the frustration setting in too deep or too fast. Or both.'

'Do you know what I saw?' Dinesh asked.

'Go on,' Liz asked gently.

'I could see someone with a massive emotional orientation change. What meant something in the past now meant nothing, and new things were taking their place. He'd never in the past be concerned over a pattern of flashing lights. I've known him too long for that. What I saw was something new – something different. Those lights wouldn't have meant a thing in the past, but to him today it meant everything – almost as if it meant the world to him and he'd be lost without it – as if there was no point unless he could solve it...'

'That could also be traits of Aspergers. Many Asperger people like things to have a point,' Liz agreed. 'But what we see as being pointless can be the total opposite in others.'

'Look, it's early days yet,' Ed said tiredly. 'This can just be the result of the experience Adam's been through. We can't be sure of anything until we've seen more. Dinesh, will you keep up those notes?'

'No problem, you told me to so I will.'

'Now, Liz and I will meet every day after Adam's done the daily video so bring those notes up with you, and we'll go through everything we see. Liz, you OK with that?'

'Yes...yes, that's fine.'

'Liz, you alright?'

'Yes,' was the hesitant reply. 'I'm just thinking of how Adam will be doing in that library tonight.'

'It's tomorrow that worries me,' Dinesh said. 'What'll happen about that essay if it's late?'

'Look, people, there's too much stress going on in here,' interrupted Ed. 'Let's chill out. It's been a hard day for all of us, and we've all seen things today that nobody else has ever seen before. We've got to go and sleep on it and let things take their course and we'll sort tomorrow's problems out tomorrow. Right?'

Liz and Dinesh nodded.

Chapter Nine

The library was the quietest room in the university. Despite it being full of students, reading, selecting books, sitting at computers and comparing notes, there was only the occasional click of a computer mouse, a low whisper or a soft thump of a book being put back on the shelf which punctuated the silence. But the registration area was dominated by noise – for all students, there was the usual frenzy of getting the right books out before closing time. However for Adam, the pressure was doubled through the fact that his assignment was due the very next day and he had only just realised what books he needed in the first place.

He had worked hard, going through the reading list, searching for the areas and numbers, and making sure he had the maximum amount the library let him have out at any one time. He'd done as much work in the library itself as he could – starting the assignment off, taking notes, references, information – but he knew that some books he would still need to take with him to make a really good job of the essay. He'd got the books with no problem at all. But he was nervous in the registration area. He'd never even taken out a book before, having in the past relied solely on Brad and Amy and the books they'd brought out, so he needed to familiarise himself with the registration procedure. A terrible moment of panic engulfed him as he realised he needed his library card to take books out and he thought he'd left it at home – after all, he'd never needed it before – but somehow, after a great deal of fumbling around in pockets and wallets, he'd found it lurking at the bottom of his rucksack.

To his surprise, he found the queuing stressful. This was something he'd never discovered before. The pressure of people around him, the lack of personal space, the constant chatter in the queue, the shuffling of books and bags – all this seemed to overload him. Even smells such as that of the deodorant worn by the girl in front of him seemed to be amplified a hundred times. He was conscious of his heart thumping, his temper rising, sweat breaking out, each minute worse than the last. *Why am I getting angry?* He had hardly ever been angry in his life, and yet here it was, happening in a simple queue at the library!

When he got to the end of the queue, he had trouble trying to understand the instructions to automatically register the books on his ticket. He eventually worked it out after a great deal of fuss – but for some strange reason he couldn't ask the staff for help. The self-confidence which hitherto was such a strong part of his personality existed no more.

There was something deep down, almost like a voice – it was saying - *Don't ask anyone. They'll think you're an idiot. Look how fast the others are doing it. Embarrassing yourself in front of a stranger! Stay away from strangers and then they won't know what a moron you really are. Don't be a fool.* This voice in his head began to recur, almost like a looping stuck tape in his brain – on and on and on...it took him a long while to register all the books, even after learning how to do it, because that loop wouldn't stop playing, that tape wouldn't turn off...

When ready, he loaded the rucksack and swung it over his shoulder. Making sure he'd got the card, he thought about the assignment.

I've no notes to guide me – how am I going to plan this?

The worry consumed him to the extent he was just heading towards the doors with his head down, deep in thought – and inadvertently bumped straight into Dr Hewitt, his lecturer!

Adam was startled, and stepped backwards in shock. But equally surprised was Dr Hewitt.

'Adam! How are things?'

Adam found himself having trouble concentrating on what his lecturer was asking him. It was as if his brain was having problems changing gear. The vague question was leaving him without a reply. *Why can't I think quickly about this?*

'Er...fine, thanks,' Adam answered after a long pause.

'It's not often I get to see you in here!' his lecturer commented with a rare smile.

Adam stared – usually the presence of Dr Hewitt meant another lecture for being late, a face white with anger, another lost temper – but here he was complimenting him! He took another step back.

'Well,' he slowly replied, trying to find a satisfactory explanation, 'It's just that your essay is due tomorrow and I'm making sure it will be ready on time.'

Hewitt looked surprised at this; after all, he had lost count of the times he had told Adam off for being late, and here he was trying to get an assignment done on time! He has the discretion not to comment on it or to press the point, but just smiled back.

'See you tomorrow morning, Adam. My seminar is at ten o'clock, and then you can hand your essay in. I'm looking forward to it.'

'Thanks,' was the reply.

Adam left the building, leaving a surprised lecturer looking after him.

Chapter Ten

Adam was back in the lab. After a long night doing the essay till 3am in the morning, Adam had been bundled out of his bed by both his mother and the alarm clock, got himself ready and organised to the best of his ability and was on time reporting for the daily video log with Liz and Ed in the lab. As soon as a file came up, with 'Video three – Wednesday' as its heading, Adam spoke into the microphone.

'It's day two of the video log. It's 0928hrs now. I was studying late last night. I've got an essay to give in to Dr Hewitt this morning after his seminar at ten. I saw him yesterday as he was leaving the library. He told me he was looking forward to my essay; I just hope it's good enough for him.'

Thoughts and memories of the library came into his mind. Liz gently prompted him to continue.

'How did you feel?'

Adam was about to react with 'What's the point?' at the mention of feelings, but hurriedly swallowed a surge of annoyance before settling down to continue.

'Well, first the cafe...Brad yesterday said something about me being a head-case. I'm sure he thinks I'm strange. I can't fit in any more, but I don't know why. It's as if there's something different about me, something which I can't explain, and which wasn't there before...'

He sadly looked down at his desk. He felt the kind hand of Liz on his shoulder.

'Then there's the library. Why was I angry in that queue? It was strange but when I was queuing up to take the books out I was feeling angry because of the queue. I'm not sure why. It was moving fast enough, I wasn't waiting too long, and nobody else seemed to be stressed about it but I was. It was weird.

'Then there was all the trouble trying to get the books to register. Why are those instructions so complicated? It took me ages to figure what they were asking me to do. I couldn't make out if the automation system wanted my card first, or the books first – everything got mixed up. And it took ages to sort out – I was frightened of holding the whole queue up.

'And another thing puzzled me – I saw several members of staff going round but I hadn't the confidence to ask anyone. I can usually go straight up to a stranger and ask them anything. But I couldn't. I was afraid. It was fear...but it was more than fear, it was like a panic! As if to speak to a stranger was wrong, what they would think, as if they'd laugh, call me names because I'd be an idiot and I don't want them to think I'm an idiot...' Adam was sweating again, his voice speeding up again as in the previous recording session, but this time with fear. 'What would they think – a student who's been there since October and couldn't even take a book out of the library?' He stopped to catch his breath, turning pale at the thought, gripping the microphone harder, eyes round, beginning to tremble. 'What would they say after I'd gone?' His voice began shaking. 'What – what would they be thinking? This idiot – this idiot at their library who - who couldn't...couldn't even sort his books out! They'd be telling their mates, telling them – you know? Telling them, talking about me online, talking about me, talking...talking...'

'Hey, slow down some!' called Ed from one of the monitors; clearly the readings were showing clear signs of severe strain on Adam's part. 'Relax. Deep breath now. It's OK.'

Adam's sweaty hands slowly released their grip on the mic.

'That'll do,' said Liz. 'That's enough for today.'

'I'm not finished yet! Something else happened, please let me finish this!' Adam was desperate. *I must finish what I'm saying – I must finish what I've started -*

'Slow down,' advised Ed. 'You slow down now.'

Adam tried his best to relax, his face pale as he concentrated on fighting with the fear, grappling with his feelings, struggling to get the words out. *I must say it; I can let nothing stand in my way -*

'Then - then as I was leaving...err...leaving the library, I ran into Dr Hewitt as I said before, but I was thinking about the essay and then he asked me about things, how are things, or something like that - and I couldn't reply! I don't know why – it was as if the question was mixed up or something, there was no detail to it so I couldn't find an answer because the words were tangled up - and for some reason I couldn't concentrate, it felt strange. It was as if I had to drag myself back through time to answer. He was talking to me, and I had to slow down, I had to think first before I could reply to him! It was strange. I couldn't think straight. Not until I had to slow down first...it was strange...so strange...'

'Now, that really is enough,' Liz said sternly. Adam looked up as she turned the recording off. 'No more. Give yourself a minute to calm down then off you go. It's time you got off to that seminar of yours. Dr Hewitt will be waiting. You be there on time.'

'I just want him to see this essay,' Adam replied, his colour returning to his cheeks. 'I've worked all night on this. I want it to be right.'

'I'm sure he'll be surprised,' agreed Liz.

Adam left with a smile.

Liz turned round. 'Ed, we are meeting in ten minutes in my office. Dinesh, can you make it?'

'Yes I can, as long as it's not too long, my first lecture today is at eleven.'

'That's fine. And bring your notes.'

Chapter Eleven

Liz was waiting in her office for Dinesh to organise his notes. 'Ed will be here as soon as he's satisfied the video recordings have taken properly.'

'I'm ready now,' Dinesh said, organising the notes.

'Right, so what's your opinion of Adam and his experiences in the library?'

'Firstly, I know Adam enough to know he'd never get upset in a queue. I've lost count of how many times we queued up to the cinema to see a picture and he's never been upset once.'

'Yet in the library, he was,' said Liz. 'And that queue frustrated him so much that he got angry. That's clearly not the same Adam you've known all your life.'

'What could have caused this?'

'My estimate is that it was information overload,' Liz replied. 'A queue full of people – there'd be noises, smells, the pressure of people and lack of personal space - everything would be overwhelming – and then worrying about what to do when you're next in line at the counter. If that was put on top of all those incoming emotions, it would have very likely caused an overload and resulted in stress, which maybe would develop into frustration, which then could cause anger.'

'And the registration instructions – Adam didn't understand those. Also he didn't ask for help, he'd usually go straight up to somebody!'

'I'll check those instructions myself,' Liz replied. 'If they are too vague – as I think they could be – and what he has to do isn't in a logical order, then that could explain why he couldn't understand them. Many people with learning difficulties – some Asperger people for example - need everything in order showing exactly what they need to do, and be given time to follow the instructions one by one to make sure they are right. They like routines and plenty of detail.'

'But why didn't he ask someone to help him out?'

'He mentioned panic – as if everyone would think him an idiot for asking. Hi Ed!'

'That's sorted out, the recording's OK.' Ed took a seat. 'I take it we're discussing Adam.'

'And the library,' Liz replied. 'And the lack of confidence.'

'You know, that's the biggest thing I've ever seen. This week I've seen someone who's really confident lose it all the following day. You'd never know it was the same person, looking at those videos.'

'He's changed so much,' Dinesh agreed. 'In the past he wouldn't care what people thought of him for asking. In fact he used to deliberately do crazy stuff and play the fool on purpose to get attention! He wouldn't care who saw him or what they thought of him. He'd do it just to get a laugh.'

'That is totally different to his reaction at the library. Adam recognised that he needed help, but didn't ask anyone for fear of how they'd react,' Liz cut in. 'This could help us understand why some people never disclose their learning difficulties for fear of ridicule or similar. If everyone else in that queue was happily following the instructions with no problems, and didn't need to ask anyone for assistance, then Adam would have been the only one who needed any help. To ask would have singled him out.'

'He'd sooner cope alone and struggle,' said Ed. 'In order to be just the same as everyone else.'

'Except the others weren't struggling and that's the difference,' said Liz. 'It was important to Adam that nobody knew he was struggling at all, not even the staff. He would blend in with the others. That was, for him, top priority – to remain unnoticed, to disappear into that queue, to be just like one of the others. He'd do this to avoid people laughing at him, name-calling, things like this – that was more important than even getting the help he needed.'

'Wow, that's strong,' exclaimed Ed.

'He's a strong person,' Dinesh agreed.

Chapter Twelve

At five to ten, Adam was sitting down with the other students in Dr Hewitt's office. Hewitt gave him a look of surprise, but said nothing. Brad also gave him a look of surprise and opened his mouth to say something – but Amy, sitting next to him, gave him an elbow and a warning look and he closed his mouth at once.

Adam looked totally indifferent, as if this was just another seminar, another meeting, another session in the office, another day at uni. There was no hint of any emotion in his face of any kind.

'Right,' Hewitt began, precisely on the stroke of ten. 'Thank you all for coming, and those of you who handed your hard copies of your assignments in to the undergraduate office before today will have them marked up by the end of next week. Everyone else, the deadline for hard copies is midday today, and they will take another four days at least before they're marked. But emailed copies to myself and personal tutors should all have reached me by now.'

Brad started grinning. He looked across the room at Adam, trying to catch his eye. But Adam looked totally serious, listening to every word his lecturer was saying, with a level of attention which neither Brad nor Amy had ever seen before.

During the hour-long seminar that followed, Brad was concentrating on Adam far more than Hewitt. He was noticing changes in him – the fact that he was following the material and taking notes. Taking notes! At one point he even asked Hewitt a question about a phrase he didn't understand – this amazed Brad, who knew that phrase and had known it since he was a child. He grinned again when Adam asked what it meant.

Amy was also watching Adam – but seeing other changes. She noticed how difficult it was for him to keep up with the pace, and the fact that the notes he was writing were scribbled at high speed so he could keep up. She noticed when Adam asked about the phrase – but she saw his confused look and heard his low, faltering, monotone voice as the question was asked. All the confidence had gone – the Adam she knew had gone. She was astounded as to how much effort he needed now just to ask a simple question – it was as if all the energy drained out of his body in seconds while he was saying it. She also saw how tired Adam was after asking – how he slumped back into his chair and sighed deeply, all his strength gone. This was a different person completely. She shivered.

For Adam, the hour took as much energy out of him as any football game would if it had a marathon run on the top. *I must concentrate...I must keep up.* And that turn of phrase, having to ask what it meant! *Why can't I understand it? Everyone else did!*

'Right, everyone,' Hewitt concluded as the clock approached eleven, 'If you have any questions, I'll be in my office at the times shown on the door, and the next time I see you will be at the main lecture in the hall next week.' As everyone began to pack away, he turned to Adam. 'Adam – I would just like a word with you after the others have gone.'

Brad smiled and gave Amy a nudge. 'This is it!' he said excitedly.

'Come on!' Amy was on her feet.

'I'm gonna hang on.'

'You can't!'

'I'm not gonna miss this!'

Amy dragged Brad out of the office. They were the last to go, leaving Hewitt and Adam alone.

'Right, Adam,' Hewitt began, but he was interrupted by the loud bleep of the telephone. 'One minute.'

He picked up the phone and his face instantly grew angry.

'Atkins! I've told you before – what are you going on about? I can't hear you. Speak up, man! What? Say again?' He turned to Adam and shook his head. Adam waited, both motionless and emotionless.

Hewitt stormed down the phone. 'Bronchitis - what do you mean, you've got bronchitis? How the devil can a little cold turn into bronchitis? Come on, man. It's this weekend. Don't you dare let any of us down; we have worked too hard for this. Do you hear me, Atkins? You'd better be there or else!' He slammed the receiver down, and then took a couple of minutes to bring his temper back under control.

Adam stayed still, waiting for his lecturer to speak to him, and remaining silent until he was spoken to. *I don't know when it's my turn to speak – I must wait for my turn.* He thought at one point he could hear a small noise outside the office door, but he listened for another one and it didn't return.

'My apologies again, that's the same man I was angry at on the phone yesterday,' Hewitt explained. 'First a cold and now he's saying it's bronchitis – it's just an excuse, nothing but lack of commitment. Honestly.'

Adam nodded, faintly remembering the first call the day before. 'You were saying there was a big event or something?'

'Yes, that's right, this weekend. There's about fifteen of us involved and we have worked hard all winter trying to get everything right. This is the first event we'll be all together at and now this happens. We have the final rehearsal on Friday night; he'd better be ready by then.'

'I hope he will be.'

'Anyway, I wanted to speak to you about your essay. I'm impressed. Not only was it done on time but the content is much improved from your previous work.'

'Thanks.' Adam responded with no emotion.

'I'm serious. I love the way you've explained the concepts in this way. I've never known anyone explain it so well – not a first-year, anyway.'

Adam wasn't used to being complimented and it took a few seconds for him to figure out how to respond. 'It was – well, so logical to me. That's why I wrote it the way I did. It just seemed so straightforward.'

'I'll get back to you after I've had a proper read of this.' Hewitt was smiling now. Adam had never known him to smile at him before. 'How about coming to see me tomorrow for tutorial?'

'Yes, I can do that as long as it's in the morning,' Adam replied. 'I've got football tonight, then tomorrow I need to do the video first thing as usual in the lab. I've a full lecture with Dr Parker in the afternoon but I can see you in the morning after the video, if you are available in the morning.'

'Yes, I am,' Hewitt replied. 'Have you recovered from doing all that hard work?'

'Yes, thank you.'

'I know one thing – that effort was well worth it, seeing the difference it has made to your work! See you tomorrow.'

'Thank you.' As Adam made ready to leave, he heard another noise from behind the office door, a bit like soft running feet. However, when he opened the door he saw nothing and nobody. He made his way to the lifts, pleased with how the morning was going.

A door slowly opened after the lift doors closed, and two faces peered out.

'Well, that didn't go as expected, did it, Brad?'

'No, it didn't,' was the angry reply. 'He's acting smart now, trying to turn himself into a teacher's pet so the uni will think he's a genius and give him awards and stuff. But I can see straight through him, the little creep.'

'Look, just forget about it, OK?'

'No way. That's out the question, Amy. I'm going to get him, and crush him, and show everyone what an act he's putting on. He'd better watch out, he'd better, because I'm gonna have him.'

Chapter Thirteen

The football changing rooms usually were a hive of activity. It would be crammed with noisy shouts, the stench of sweaty bodies and even sweatier shirts, muddy shorts and shoes being pulled off, laughter, chatter, and the steam from the shower room.

But not now. Not this time.

The only activity there was breathing. Slow, deep, trembling breaths, air blowing noisily through gloved hands.

Where did I go wrong? What happened?

Adam was alone. Totally alone in the world.

In the past, he'd be enjoying the game with the team, out there in goal, the fans cheering with every save he made.

But not now. Not this time.

The shouts of his teammates, together with the roar of supporters at the football match could be heard outside. This only added to Adam's sense of abandonment.

Why? Why me?

He was sitting on a bench, still wearing his goalkeeper's football kit. There was nobody to talk to and nothing to do. Nothing to do but wait...just wait.

His head was in his gloved hands, then he raised his head; the look on his face showed total despair, disappointment, even shock. He then buried his face back into his gloves, as if he was still trying to hang on to the only proof of evidence he had that he could play football. After all, that's what he'd been doing for years, and everyone loved him for it.

In the past he'd be holding cups aloft with cheering crowds around him.

But not now. Not this time.

Adam was now wondering if he could even play football at all or if he even had done in the past.

Where did I go wrong? What happened?

Loud cheers now could be heard; Adam looked up once again, conscious of the match ending. He sighed deeply.

Why? Why me?

He could hear a large tramping of feet coming closer and closer, and his teammates entered, Brad, the captain, at the head of the line. He wasted no time, but went straight for Adam.

'What the hell were you playing at?'

There was no reply, no motion, no sound answered him.

Brad walked quickly towards Adam, and pulled his gloves down sharply away from his face. He looked up in response, but still gave no reply.

'I asked you a question! What the hell's wrong with you? You were letting every ball in!'

Still no reply.

'You're a bloody idiot, that's what you are! You moron! I don't know why the hell I let you play in the first place! You can't even catch a ball!'

The other members of the team were looking round as they were undressing, sweat on their bodies, disgust on their faces.

Brad turned his face away from Adam, facing his teammates.

'This prat here' – he pointed to Adam but did not face him – 'can't even catch a ball properly.'

Some of the team shook their heads, others looked down; a few were smirking.

'And all he can do is sit and cry!'

All eyes were on Adam now.

What happened out there?

'I'm...sorry,' Adam began. 'I – I don't know. I just don't know what...'

'He's sorry.' Brad scowled at the team.

The sad face once again buried itself in the gloved hands.

'He's sorry!' Brad was sneering now. 'Sorry! Sorry for being such a prat? Sorry that thanks to you we haven't got a decent goalie ready for the next match on Saturday? Sorry for letting everyone down? Sorry for being the fool of the whole uni?'

The face remained buried.

'I didn't hear that?'

The face and hands underwent no change.

'Still can't hear you!'

No changes. No words. There was nothing to say, no words to say it with.

There's nothing for me here now.

Brad got down on the bench, and put his face very close to Adam's gloves.

'Anybody in there?'

The response was sharp laughter from the team, but nothing from Adam.

Brad got up from the bench, and addressed the team.

'I'll tell you something.' Here he pointed to himself. 'I'm sorry. Do you believe that? He says he's sorry but it's me that's sorry. I'm sorry that I even considered letting this moron here' – he pointed to Adam – 'into our footy team.'

The team nodded in agreement.

'I'm sorry that I even set eyes on this stupid piece of shit here.' He grabbed Adam's shoulder and shook it. 'This piece of shit here! And – do you know where shit should go?'

Brad's angry face faced Adam's devastated one.

'Where should it go, Adam?' he shouted loudly into his face.

No reply.

Brad spoke softly now, his ear next to Adam's mouth.

'I said, where should it go?'

He paused, waiting for an answer, but receiving none. At this, he drew away from Adam, but was still sneering at him.

'Let me give you a clue.'

Brad grabbed Adam and pulled him straight off the bench, onto the floor; from there he got hold of one boot and began dragging him towards the toilets. At this, the team burst out laughing.

'Come on!' yelled Brad. 'Come on and help me get rid of the shit. Come on!'

Several team members now ran to join in, shouting and laughing; Adam had his arm grabbed by one of his former teammates, and his other arm pulled by two others; more were dragging him along by the other foot while Brad led them on. He was roughly flung into a cubicle, then propped up on top of a toilet; everyone was jeering, yelling in his ear, pulling him by the hair, laughing all over him.

Brad shouted above all the laughter.

'There's something I really regret now!'

The team slowly quietened down; Adam trembled on the toilet, too scared to even breathe.

'My only regret is this...that this moron has such a fat arse that I can't flush him down!'

More howls of laughter once again.

'I'd flush him down. I'd flush him so far down that he'd never be heard of again. He belongs in the sewers with all the other shit.' He grabbed Adam and shook him. 'Don't you, you moron?'

He turned to the rest of the team; Adam remained as still as he could.

'Come on.'

He gave Adam a look of complete disgust and left, the rest of the team following him.

'No...'

Adam's whole world had fallen apart, his entire life was torn to pieces; the past, once reality, was now just a dream; the present, once joyful, was now a nightmare; the future, once promising, was now almost non-existent.

What happened to my life?

He sat, a pathetic, shivering figure, on the toilet, his head still buried in his gloved hands.

Chapter Fourteen

I am in goal.

What an amazing feeling. I hear the crowd cheer me at every save.

The defenders come over and say, 'Well done, mate,' and Brad the captain comes up and gives me a pat on the back.

It's hard work even thinking a goalie could be the man of the match, but I was, several times.

I can smell the leather of those gloves. Nothing feels as good as wearing those gloves. Those gloves are me, myself, my life.

I am in goal.

The team gets ready to start the game, then the whistle blows, and there's nothing like it in the world.

Off they go. Cheers, boos, whistles, groans, that crowd can sense everything we are going through.

Then I see one of the opposing team kick the ball away through midfield. Our defenders are on it, but the oncoming player dodges his marker. He still has the ball. One of the wingers cuts in but he misses. The ball then gets passed to the opposing team's big star striker.

Another striker joins him. Will he cross the ball, or will he try a shot? Both are on side, no flags are up. One defender stands between them and me. He does his best to block the attack, but now there's only me left to defend my goal.

Then he shoots!

Up I go.

I know exactly where to leap, and at what speed. That ball doesn't have a chance against me and I know it.

My body soars. My confidence soars. Up I go with arms outstretched, gloved hands ready for anything.

The crowd watches with baited breath, hearts in mouths – will that ball go in? The opposing fans want it to, our own fans don't, but both sets of fans are silent, waiting, faces covered by hands which are in turn covered by woollen mittens and gloves.

The ball comes down. Down...down...straight into my goalkeeper's gloves, leather against leather. I bring it down, curling it under my body as I reach the ground, so nobody can retrieve it.

I've got it.

That's my ball.

Nobody else's.

The crowd go mad, the whistle blows, up come the defence, and I see Brad out the corner of my eye running towards me in the same old way. I slowly stand as the team gathers around me, amazed at the thing I've just done.

They're laughing.

Brad's laughing.

I give him the ball.

'Where should it go, Adam?'

A sudden change of tone.

'It's here, Brad,' I reply, pointing to the ball.

'I said, where should it go?'

'It's here...'

Brad pulls me down, yelling, 'Let me give you a clue. Where should it go? Let me give you a clue. Where should it go? Let me give you a clue...'

Adam woke up suddenly, jerking himself upright in bed, sweat pouring from him.

'NOOOOOO!!!!'

Chapter Fifteen

Adam felt like death warmed up the next morning as he came in to the lab to do the daily video record. Liz and Dinesh saw the difference in him as he slowly dragged himself into the room; his head was down, as he walked slowly to the video monitor and mic without a single word, not even a nod or any sign of making contact with anyone else. Even Joe stuck his head out the door of the computer room, wondering why the lab had suddenly fallen silent.

'Adam,' Liz was very concerned. 'What's wrong?'

There was no answer, just the thump of a rucksack being flung onto a desk and the creak of a chair. He pulled the mic towards him.

'Adam...'

'Just tell me when to start,' a muffled, monotone voice replied from a head which rested in his folded arms across the desk.

'Adam...'

'Just start it!' Adam jerked his head up in sudden anger. 'Please,' he added as an afterthought.

'OK,' Liz answered, seeing pure pain etched into Adam's face. She continued with loading a file with 'Video Four – Thursday' and signalling him to go ahead.

Adam paused before starting. *Why can't I find the right words?* It was hard for anyone to know what to say when their whole world's falling to pieces. Adam sighed, and brought the mic further towards him.

'It's hard to know what to say today,' he began after a minute or so. 'First I've got to apologise to everyone for losing my temper just now. I've never done that before, but it was just stress, I guess.'

He folded his arms across the desk again and buried his head.

'It's yesterday,' he went on, his voice again sounding muffled as his face was still buried. 'I've no idea what's going on. I can't play football anymore. It was everything, that football, it was everything to me - and now it's gone.'

He slowly raised his head and his eyes met those of Liz.

'I've been kicked out the team, and Brad's not speaking to me. It was terrible. I played in goal and I couldn't catch the ball. Then they replaced me on the pitch, and when the team came in...it was terrible,' he said, conscious of his need to change the subject. 'I'm glad Amy is on my degree course because otherwise I wouldn't have any idea about what to do. I'd have nobody to talk to.'

He paused for a few seconds before continuing.

'Why can't I play in goal anymore? What happened, what did I do wrong? I tried to catch the ball, I couldn't catch the ball. Why couldn't I catch the ball?'

He looked up angrily.

'I did all I could,' he continued, his temper rising. 'I did all they asked me to do, I went in goal and went for the ball, but for some stupid reason I couldn't catch it, I couldn't save it, what's wrong with me? What the hell is wrong with me?'

'It's OK.' Liz's soft voice was there, preventing the anger worsening. 'Tell us about today. What will happen today?'

'Today...'

He paused, trying to think straight. He found it hard to change the subject. Liz had to ask him again a few times before he responded.

'I've got a tutorial with Dr Hewitt today, straight after I've finished in here. It's the first time I've ever booked a tutorial since I've been here, but Dr Hewitt wants to see me. He says it's something about my essay. I hope he doesn't get angry with me. He has a terrible temper. I hope he won't think I'm an idiot. Brad thinks I'm an idiot.'

Adam's head fell again into his folded arms.

'I'm so stupid. I let down the whole team because I'm such an idiot. If Dr Hewitt thinks I'm an idiot too then I've let down the whole university.'

Liz's hand came to rest on his shoulder.

'I can't think what to say anymore. I have to go to tutorial.'

He left the lab without looking at anyone, and without saying a word.

Liz went over to Dinesh, who was studying the monitor responses. 'I want your notes brought up here right now. I'll call Ed. Ten minutes, my office.'

Chapter Sixteen

'That's one thing we didn't count on.' Liz began, when Ed and Dinesh arrived.

'The impaired psychomotor reactions?' Dinesh asked. 'The problem he was having in goal?'

'Yes,' Liz sighed. 'In some special needs people, such as those with dyspraxia, their psychomotor co-ordination skills can be weak and they need a lot of practice and support techniques to get right. This has happened to Adam.'

'And that's definitely due to the experiment and not some kind of side-effect?'

'It's real all right,' Ed agreed.

'Well then,' Dinesh looked enthusiastic, 'this is good because it gives us something we can use, something we can observe developing over the next few days. I'll be able to watch Adam, take some more notes, and then we can...'

'Feel free to take notes, Dinesh,' Liz replied sadly, 'but I'm thinking on personal lines now. His football was the only thing that Adam really lived for – and now it's gone. This experiment has killed the one thing he lived for – the thing he was most passionate about.'

Dinesh looked back at Liz in shock.

'Can this problem be overcome?'

'You mean, could Adam be trained again to be in goal?'

'Yes,' Dinesh replied, 'When he goes back to how he was, at the end of the experiment, will he be able to do it again?'

'I expect so. It's a good thing that this experiment was timed to be for just a few days. God knows how Adam would react if this experiment was to be permanent!'

'So there's no need to worry,' Dinesh replied optimistically.

'But what about everyone else – those with this type of condition from the word go?' butted in Ed. 'After all, this experiment was meant to help these people!'

'It'll take a lot of training and practice but it can be done,' Liz answered. 'But the main problem is time – it takes, on average, many times longer to learn a co-ordination skill with a psychomotor problem. Therefore whoever is doing the training needs to be supportive, patient, and allow far longer in terms of time for a standard to be reached.'

'So it's about time? The longer the better, that kind of thing?'

'Time's a big factor but there's more to it than just time itself,' Liz replied. 'Some skills training could be useful to a trainer - skills such as therapy training. There could be special exercises between training sessions which could be needed, to help the co-ordination become perfect. Muscle memory, that kind of issue. Then there's confidence building – look how Adam was blaming himself over and over, asking what was wrong with him. That's very common. Slow, sure steps – and each time the person gets it right, they need to be told, otherwise there's a risk of low self-esteem setting in and worsening as time goes on.'

'At least Adam won't have to go through all that.'

'I'm just wondering what Adam will do next,' mused Liz.

'How do you mean?'

'If he's got traits of Asperger syndrome then if there's a personal passion, then it's deep, it's strong, it's like part of that person's soul,' Liz replied. 'And there's a chance that Adam will find something out there that's new, something to fill the huge hole that the football has left behind. Dinesh, keep those notes to hand – you may need them.'

Chapter Seventeen

Adam went from the lab straight to Dr Hewitt's office. He was fighting with his emotions on the way up – he had never been rejected before at anytime, anywhere, and the fact he had been rejected by his best friend, and at his sport which in the past he'd excelled at so much, added more trauma to the upset.

Now he had to get ready to face Dr Hewitt again. *What a morning. What a week. I wish I had never done this stupid experiment; all it's done is to get me into trouble.*

A familiar angry voice reached his ears – another phone call, which clearly was the wrong person calling at the wrong time.

Just like me, Adam thought, and shuddered.

When the voice eventually stopped, Adam gave a small knock at the door.

'Come in!'

Adam entered, opened his mouth to say hello – and closed it again when he saw the familiar white, angry face of his lecturer.

'Adam, thank you for coming up,' Hewitt began. 'My apologies for that phone call. You know who it was?'

Adam guessed that it was likely the same person who had rang before; however he couldn't think of the name. 'The - the one who had a cold?' he stammered out.

'Yes, Atkins,' Hewitt replied. 'That's this weekend's event in jeopardy. He can't make it, too ill, unbelievable. Anyway, what are your thoughts on your essay?'

'I'm not sure, I spent a lot of time on it though – at the library, when I saw you, then I borrowed some books to do some work at home and was on it till gone three in the morning.'

'Well, I must say it was worth every minute you spent. In all the years I've taught this particular module, I've never known a first-year to be able to produce an essay of this quality. They either stray from the question topic or don't go into detail enough. You've put a great deal of effort into this. Well done.'

Adam just stared back, totally unused to praise from his lecturer. 'Er...thanks!'

'But why were you unsure about your thoughts on the essay?'

'Well...everything else has gone wrong this week so I was expecting that to have gone wrong too... It's just things that happen to me, all these bad things.'

'You think too negatively.'

'If you'd have gone through everything going wrong in a week then you'd be thinking negatively too.'

'What's happened?'

Adam decided to tell the whole story. 'You know I had football last night? Well, I was chucked out the uni team because I couldn't catch the ball – I play in goal, you know – I mean, I did play in goal. I keep forgetting I don't play anymore.'

Hewitt looked sad as Adam continued, head down.

'It's me. I'm just stupid, I wish I wasn't. Brad was my best mate, he was team captain and he threw me out, it was my fault for not being able to play. Then there were him and the team calling me names after the game. Then I had a nightmare last night about it. Then there was the video this morning, when I had to mention it all over again. I'm just so stupid, I think I'll always be stupid - it's my lot in life. I hate myself.'

Adam was suddenly lost in his emotions. He had never felt such a depth of sadness before.

It just isn't fair.

He slowly looked up at Hewitt.

'I hate my head. It has no brain in it anymore. I'm useless. I can't even catch a ball.' He strode over towards Hewitt's desk, and, reaching up, took down from the shelf the strange black helmet which his lecturer had defended so vigorously from him a few days prior. 'My head is like this helmet.'

'In what way?' Hewitt was standing still this time, making no move to rescue his precious helmet from him.

'It's empty. Just like this helmet is empty, so my head is, because there's no brain in it. My head's like that, my skull's like that. It's the nearest I can describe it. But the difference is that this helmet is special, even though it is empty, it has something in it which I can't describe...'

Adam held the helmet with great care, in stark contrast to the first time when he picked it up. But now he could see it in a different way. There were things in that helmet now – things he couldn't see before – things which amazed him, yet things he could never explain. He couldn't find the words. He'd forgotten about comparing that helmet to his own head – this helmet now held a fascination for him, something deep, something intangible, but present all the same. He could now see more in it than he ever could before. Hewitt noticed this at once.

'Adam,' Hewitt asked, 'What's changed about that helmet since the first time you saw it?'

'I can see its detail,' he replied. 'I can see the time that someone took to create it. I can see that it's not a toy; it's been specially modified and designed. There's a strange red insignia on it. Someone's weathered it to make it look worn, and it's had padding put in,' he continued, turning it over, 'and – well, I can appreciate it more, I guess.'

Adam had the sudden urge to apologise. He looked at Hewitt.

'I'm sorry about before,' he said, 'I shouldn't have acted the way I did, and I shouldn't have called it a toy.'

'No you shouldn't,' Hewitt replied, 'but you can see now what it is in reality. You weren't able to do that before the experiment. Do you realise you can see detail now, and show more respect for things that belong to other people? If that were not true, I'd have snatched it away from you, just like I did before! But now, look – I know it's safe in your hands.'

'I think it's amazing,' Adam replied dreamily. 'I wish I could hide in this.'

'Hide?'

'Yes,' Adam replied emphatically. 'In this helmet nobody knows who it is underneath when it's on.' He paused. 'Can I put it on? I promise I'll be careful.'

'Certainly, try it.'

Adam put it on with extreme care, then slowly looked around the office, getting used to the weight on his head and the restricted and darkened vision. It excited him – he was hidden now, and all emotion and feeling he ever felt while that helmet was on would be hidden also. It was hard to tell Hewitt exactly how he was feeling.

I can face the world in this. I'm not afraid to.

He began slowly walking around the room with it on.

'You see? Nobody knows it's me. I can hide myself in here and nobody will even guess it's me. I can disappear. All I want to do is disappear. Brad wouldn't find me in here; neither would any of the other guys who called me names last night. I'd be safe in one of these. Well hidden, in here I'm hidden from that world out there and the people who hate me.'

Hewitt looked on, watching with increasing interest.

'Go on.'

Adam stopped. 'What do you mean?'

'Tell me more about how it feels to be hidden. You mention the helmet protects you from the negatives, such as the world, and hateful people; but what about the positives?'

'Positives?'

'Yes, the positives of being hidden where nobody can see you. You have the helmet on. What of your emotions?'

'Where nobody can see me...well...' Adam began. He looked back at Hewitt who smiled and nodded.

'Go on. How do you feel if you're somewhere nobody else can see you?'

'If nobody can see me I can be myself.'

'Exactly!' Hewitt responded at once. 'Think, think it through...'

'Well...I can be myself, I can think what I want, nobody can see how I'm feeling, I can be my true self in there! I can disguise aspects of myself I don't want others to see and I can bring out everything I do want people to see. I can be me, have the confidence to be me.'

He took the helmet off, but still held it with great care. Hewitt gently took it from him.

'Now you have it. You now know the reason why many people, myself included, love cosplay so much.' Adam looked surprised at the unfamiliar phrase; Hewitt saw the confused look and explained. 'It's when a person plays a character out of a film, or comic book, or TV, or similar. I find it works well if the character I play is like my true self in reality.'

'So who do you play?' Adam looked down at the helmet his lecturer was holding. 'Which character is this?'

'It's the helmet of Kyrah – that's his title; it means 'the Dark Master' - called Gandoren from the planet Arani. I guess,' he added, looking at Adam's confused face, 'that you've never heard of him?'

'No, I haven't.'

'There are two combat forces from two different worlds that coordinate an attack on another planet to get the Crystal of Life returned to their solar system after it was stolen. Have you ever read 'Vengeance of the Tribes?'

'No.'

'It's one of a trilogy of books about the Vorna galaxy.'

'So you play this character from a book?'

'That's right.'

The old Adam would have laughed out loud; the new Adam was fascinated by the concept. 'You have the costume...everything?'

'Yes, I do,' was the smiling reply. 'It's the only time I can be my true self – where a temper like mine becomes natural for the character, since anger is so much part of the Kyrah character.'

'That's amazing. But why is the helmet here?'

'Because the electronics department are helping with a new voice-changing unit,' Hewitt replied, turning the helmet over so Adam could see. 'You see, with a microphone and an amplifier, coupled with a speaker in the right place, it can be possible to replicate the voice of a character. The old one packed up last week and I wanted to see if they could run a new one for this weekend.'

'This weekend – you mean that – '

'Yes. That group I spoke of before – the group of fifteen of us who have been practising all winter – we are a group of Vorna Galaxy cosplayers. We do shows and performances, like parties and suchlike. This weekend we are doing an appearance at the local comic con.'

'What's one of those?' Adam had never heard of these before.

'Comic con – a comic convention. They are held all over the country now, very popular. People dress up in costume – that's cosplay – as characters from film, comics or TV. Some get thousands through the doors. Our battle show, set on Arani, has been very popular in the past, some of the comic cons let us have our own place in the hall so we can perform for the crowds.' Hewitt looked with pride at his helmet. 'What we are performing is the first battle of Arani. Kyrah Gandoren is the Dark Master in the battle, of course. He's mostly independent, he's not part of the Aranian army. There are two Kyerna – Dark Protectors, who are almost like his apprentices only they take a much deeper role. He's fighting against the fierce, aggressive warriors from the planet Kosa, led by their chiefs, and combat soldiers from the planet Zenar.'

Adam was trying his best to keep up with everything Hewitt was saying. Hewitt sensed the loss of concentration and stopped.

'Are you with me so far?'

'Er...well, you're Gandoren, there are some warriors and combat soldiers and then you mentioned someone else...'

'Kyerna, the Dark Protectors. We always have two; they are the two that are chosen by Gandoren for training to be the next Dark Master. They always fight alongside him, and wear red robes as part of their costumes.' He went over to his desk, put down the helmet and brought a photograph out from one of the drawers. 'This is what they look like.'

Adam looked at the bright crimson robes, the smooth, shiny helmet with the black visor; he could feel a smile slowly breaking out.

I could hide myself in there. I could disappear. Completely.

'But we've now got a bit of a problem. You know...'

Adam was still totally lost in the photo.

'Are you paying attention?'

'Sorry, Dr Hewitt. I was just thinking how brilliant it would be to play in this.'

'Well, as I was saying, we have a bit of a problem. You remember Atkins? Bronchitis?'

'Yes.' Adam couldn't easily forget those angry phone calls.

'Well, he was due to play one of our Dark Protectors. Now he's suddenly decided to be ill just before our show weekend. Now we've only one ready. We need two, no question about it.' He stopped, suddenly recollecting what Adam had just said. 'You were saying?'

'Sorry?'

'What did you say about this?'

'I'm sorry; it was just that I was thinking out loud.'

'But you were saying you'd like to play?'

Adam looked down at the photo again. 'I would like to. It would be amazing.' Then his face fell. 'But what am I talking about? I can't even play football anymore so how on earth could I do anything like this?'

Hewitt smiled. 'The person playing football was you. In this costume, you're no longer you – you're playing a character. And this character is confident, he stands tall, and he's protective of his Dark Master, Gandoren. Could you be a character like that?'

'I'd like to be.' His face brightened. 'I'd love to do it!'

'How tall are you?'

'I'm just over six foot.'

'We will need to measure you up with your boots on. We need the two of you to be tall and about the same height. I'm sure if you're not tall enough, one of our group members will have some lifts.'

'Lifts?'

'Yes, small insoles to put in the boots to raise your height. Now, what are you doing tomorrow evening?'

'Not a lot. Just at home as usual. It's likely I'll be copying up the notes from Dr

Parker's lecture this afternoon and doing part of an assignment for him.'

'Well, if you're free tomorrow evening, I'll take you down to the group rehearsal. Then I'll introduce you to the members of our group, and try a costume fitting. If all goes well, then you'll be performing at our show on Saturday. How's that?'

'That'll be fantastic.'

'Excellent. Now, I want you to keep that photo and learn as much about that character as you can when you've a bit of time away from your studies.'

'Tomorrow I'll have to do a video as usual,' Adam said. 'It's part of this experiment. Am I allowed to mention this?'

'Of course you can. Not in detail otherwise everyone will know too much about what we're doing in the group and the last thing we need is people talking about our show even before they've seen it yet.'

'I'll remember; no worries.'

It was a totally different Adam who
walked out of the office, a complete contrast to
the Adam who had walked in that morning.

Chapter Eighteen

The whole lab saw the change in Adam when he walked in the next morning to do the video recording.

'Adam!' called Ed with a huge smile, running round the monitors in his usual way adjusting the machines. 'You are feeling better today!'

'Yes, thanks.'

'Did Brad let you back into the team?' Dinesh asked, coming over from the monitors, his crisp white lab coat showing up starkly against Ed's heavily soiled one.

'No,' Adam replied, sitting down in the usual familiar seat at the usual familiar desk. 'But I've got something else planned now. I'll mention it in the recording. I think you'll like it.'

Dinesh looked surprised. 'What is it?'

'I'm not allowed to tell too much about it, only a few bits.'

'Whatever it is, I've got to take notes on it for the experiment. That's part of my job. I hope that's OK.' Dinesh reached into a drawer and took out a huge sheaf of papers. 'That's what I've got already, but unlike your planned activities, these I'm not allowed to tell you about!'

'That's fine, 'Adam replied as Liz set up the mic as usual.

'Hey, that's a nice t-shirt you've got on!' she exclaimed, looking down at Adam's new shirt. It was black with stars and galaxies all over it, a stark contrast to his everlasting sports tops and football shirts he'd worn every day until that point.

'I got it last night,' Adam said proudly.

'Neat,' Dinesh commented. 'Are you turning into an astronomer? Think of that, Adam the scientist? You'll be like me soon!'

'It reminds me of this activity I'm doing. I'm looking so forward to doing it.'

'Well, now you can tell us all about it,' Liz replied, loading a file up saying 'Video Five – Friday' and giving Adam the signal to start.

It took Adam several seconds to think about what to say; after all, Hewitt had told him not to reveal too much detail...

'Well...' he began, pausing for a few seconds before continuing. 'I went up to see Dr Hewitt yesterday morning and...I'm not sure if anyone knows but Dr Hewitt is part of some group who dress in costume and do shows. I'm not sure if it's fantasy or sci-fi. But anyway, he – he's part of this group, and one of them has phoned in sick...um...and he wants me to replace him because they're doing a show on Saturday.'

He paused again, sensing the eyes of everyone else in the room burning into his back. Even Joe had his head round the door again, listening.

'Dr Hewitt has told me not to tell anyone about the show itself, as to who the characters are or anything like that. I can't say what the actual show is that we'll be doing, because I don't know that myself yet – all I know is that it's a scene from a battle which is set on another planet. It sounds really exciting. The show's going to be performed at the local comic con – I've only just learnt what one of those is.'

'How does doing all this make you feel?' asked Liz.

For the first time, Adam began to understand why Liz kept on mentioning feelings to him – and this time he had something to say, rather than just annoyance.

'It started with that helmet Dr Hewitt has in his office. I told him my head was like that helmet because it was empty – I was upset about the football.' He paused, sadness returning for a few seconds as he remembered those dreadful events a couple of nights ago.

Liz gently encouraged him. 'The helmet Dr Hewitt has. What happened?'

'I put it on, and all of a sudden there I was, totally hidden from everyone. I felt free in there.' Adam could feel the sadness leaving him even as he spoke. 'I was free to show all feelings and emotions without anyone else seeing or being aware of them. Every time I'd wear that, I would be hidden from the world, and it wouldn't matter what others said, or even what they think, because in that helmet I can be myself completely and nobody will even know.'

He looked up from the mic and smiled at Liz.

'How does performing at that con make you feel? Are you nervous? Tell us.'

Adam turned back to the mic, thinking of words to describe how he felt. *Why can't I ever find the right words?*

'I would be nervous doing this, but only if I was myself – I mean, if I was just on stage as me, or doing something as I am now. But Dr Hewitt was saying something about only the character being seen by everyone, and that character wouldn't be me. It would be someone else, which means that I would be hidden, and all my own feelings would be hidden. And because I'll be hidden, that means I'm not nervous. That's the best way that I can describe it.'

'Do you have to practise anything before Saturday?' Dinesh asked.

''Dr Hewitt told me to find out as much about the character as I could, so I've borrowed a book out the library which contains the scene we'll be acting out at the con. Also there's a rehearsal tonight which Dr Hewitt is taking me to. To be honest, I'm more nervous about that

120

than I am of the actual show, because it will be a group of strangers I've never met in my life.'

'So you're nervous because they're strangers?' asked Dinesh. He couldn't believe this, since the old Adam was confident in front of everyone, strangers included.

'A bit. I guess it's because I'm the outsider.' His face fell. 'I don't belong in that group. Everyone else will know what they're doing, and will all know each other. I don't belong in that group at all, I'm only doing this as a favour to Dr Hewitt because one of the members got sick and they needed a replacement.'

Liz tried to help him. 'Do you understand that because Dr Hewitt invited you down to the rehearsal, that his action makes you a part of that group, at least till after the show?'

'No. I can't see that at all. I won't know anyone and they don't know me. So I'm not one of them and that means I'm not a member of that group.'

'A logical train of thought in the brain. This is very common,' Liz replied. 'Dinesh, take some notes on this.'

Dinesh immediately produced pen and paper, and began scribbling away at high speed to catch up.

Ed came over, lab coat stuffed with too many wires and tools in the pockets as usual.

'Maybe I can help, Adam?'

'Ok, see if you can, because I don't understand.'

'Now, you know we're all part of this team here. Me, you, Liz, Dinesh, Joe on the computers, Dr Keller, and the technical staff. One team, you agree?'

'Yes.'

'Well, let's say I had the flu, right? I was ill, I couldn't get here one day and I asked another lecturer from the Department of Engineering to take over. He arrives in here, you see him – what would your thoughts be? Would you follow his directions as you would mine? Would Dinesh?'

'Yes, we would,' Adam agreed, looking at Dinesh nodding beside him, still taking notes.

'So there you go. If you would do that to a new person, then that new person is part of that team. Just like you tonight. You're going down to that rehearsal to replace someone else, so they'd treat you as if you were part of that group. Now can you see?'

'I can understand it more,' Adam replied, slowly thinking it through, 'but I can't apply this to myself for some reason.'

'That's low self-esteem,' Liz said. 'Low self-esteem coupled with a lack of understanding of how groups work. But when you go to that rehearsal tonight, remember what Ed said and you'll see he was right!'

Chapter Nineteen

Throughout the day at university, Adam had trouble concentrating. Regardless of where he was – the lecture hall, the library, the cafe – the same thoughts came back to haunt him.

Am I good enough? Will I be accepted as one of the group even though I'm an outsider?

It was if his mind and soul were split into two - excitement on one side and fear on the other. Half of him was desperate to play, driven by the need for him to hide in that helmet. This was coupled with a feeling he had never experienced before – the need for self-expression, the need to express his anger towards those who hated him while playing the role of a character like himself, his true self as it really was. He had an overwhelming desire to view the opposing characters in the battle scene as Brad and the members of his old football team. That incident after his last game was still fresh with him, clear as crystal, playing back at full volume in full technicolour inside his head, keeping him awake at night, appearing in his dreams. His desire to unleash his rage was intense, and he knew that only by being able to put that costume on, and be safely hidden in a helmet, could it have any chance of being satisfied in a way that the social world would approve of.

However the fearing half of his soul wanted to call time on the whole lot. He was very much afraid of being with strangers, doubtful of whether or not he would be accepted by them. What if he didn't fit in, or he was laughed at when he couldn't do something right, or stood in the wrong place at the wrong time? How would he react? Would he turn and run, or be driven by the same anger he had towards Brad? And to make matters worse his lecturer was there too – Dr Hewitt, he who had the temper of the devil himself, he who he had had so much trouble with through his first university year so far – he who was giving him his first praise four months after his studies started.

Trying to get through the day was tough, with Brad not speaking to him or even looking in his direction. There was also a problem with terminology that he was experiencing – more and more of the words used in his lectures and seminars were becoming incomprehensible. He was now carrying two sets of notes with him – the first was the list of notes he'd taken from the lecture content, while the second was a list of unfamiliar terms and words, spelt as best he could, for him to search online for after the lecture to find out what they meant. He couldn't ask Brad any more, and he'd considered asking Amy, but Amy was spending time with Brad so often now that it was hard for Adam to catch her on her own.

Adam followed Hewitt's instructions. He'd gone to the library during his break and researched everything he could find about what he'd called the 'first battle of Arani,' as his lecturer had described it. He'd had a look at the characters, including the one he'd be playing himself, one of the Kyerna, the Dark Protectors.

That's who I'll be. A Kyerna. A Dark Protector. I can do this, I know I can...

As the day wore on, Adam became more and more concerned about the evening rehearsal. Dr Hewitt had already emailed saying he'd meet him outside the uni cafe after the day was over, and telling him to make sure he'd eaten prior to the rehearsal to ensure he wouldn't become weak when in costume. Adam was worried by this – this new Adam was. The old Adam wouldn't have been concerned at all, being all too aware of fitness preparing for the football; but the new

Adam was doing his best to keep all thoughts of football out of his head since the memories of his last game were burning strong within him and he was doing all he could to forget so he could carry on.

At the appointed time, precise as always, Dr Hewitt was waiting outside the cafe – and a very pale Adam stumbled out through the doors.

Hewitt turned to him. 'Are you alright?'

'Just...just a bit nervous, that's all. I don't know why, maybe it's because I'm going to meet people I don't know.'

'Well, you needn't be,' Hewitt reassured him, as they walked towards the car park. 'The group knows all about you, they're great people otherwise I won't be doing all this with them in my spare time. They're very pleased that you've volunteered to fill Atkins's shoes at the last minute. Oh, that reminds me. David Atkins is a member of my staff, that's why I call him by his surname but in this group everyone's on first-name terms. Will you be alright with that?'

Adam was startled. Everyone at that university knew about how Hewitt always addressed staff by their surnames, how he hated using first names and being on first-name terms, and that nobody loved being called by his surname than Hewitt himself.

'Excuse me? The group is all on first name terms?'

'Yes, that's right. So that means, when we are at this rehearsal, and in anything to do with this group, you can call me Tony.'

'Er...Tony.'

'But only in that group, mind, nowhere else.'

'Yes, of course,' Adam replied hurriedly, wondering where on earth this group had got the power from to change someone's habit of a lifetime.

'Good.'

Adam naturally wanted to know where they were going, but overwhelming nerves and lack of confidence prevented any conversation taking place on the drive down. After about half an hour they pulled up at a large building which looked from the outside like a huge hall, where a small, dark-haired lady in black top and leggings was waiting on the steps outside.

'That's Rosa, she plays Liapi, the Kosan female lead. How much information have you found about the Vorna Galaxy?'

'I know the planets the characters are from, a few of the names, who my character is...'

'That's a start. So you know about Liapi, the character Rosa is playing?'

'Yes.'

'You'll be amazed how well Rosa performs; she has everything just right for that part.'

Adam felt his confidence fall – after all, Hewitt had found perfection in Rosa, but what about his own role? He looked unhappy as they parked, wondering if he'd done the right thing by being there at all.

Rosa ran over to the car and greeted them both with a friendly smile. 'So you are the new Kyerna?' she asked Adam in a slightly foreign accent.

'Um...only for tomorrow,' Adam blurted out, looking away, unsure of what to say in front of a complete stranger.

'We are sure you can stay longer than that!' she replied, leading the way into the hall.

Adam had never set foot in a place like this hall in his life – the nearest he'd ever got to anywhere like this was a sports pavilion where he'd be changing for the football matches. Rosa was leading the way, pointing out where all the facilities were and what would happen. Adam was amazed at her enthusiasm – she appeared to have endless energy which appeared to be bottomless.

'And by the way, I'm Rosanna Estorelli, just call me Rosa, everyone does.'

'Um...thanks, Rosa.' Adam found himself looking away again, even though he didn't mean to.

'Rosa,' Hewitt asked from behind, 'Can you introduce Adam to Sean? Adam – Sean O'Donnell plays the other Kyerna, and he'll show you the costume and how it goes on. Then when it's on, we'll do a sizing check just to see if you're the same height together.'

"*Nessun problema*, Tony. You come with me,' Rosa smiled, turning to Adam. 'Sean's down here. This way.'

They walked through several corridors, and Adam was amazed at what he was seeing in them. Against the walls there were weapons looking to Adam like long maces. A stack of short swords was packed into one corner. Bags and crates were stacked all over the floor, some piled several high, and lots of armour pieces and boots were scattered about.

Adam was also amazed at the noise. People in various states of dress or undress were wandering around, talking, and unloading packs and cases everywhere. There was the constant scraping noise from cases being pulled round on uncarpeted floors. Someone in a room was shouting for help doing up his boots, another was running in and out looking for a helmet and asking everyone else if they'd seen it. Adam could hardly concentrate on following Rosa at all – what with all the noise and action, having to clamber over scattered bags and trunks, and seeing things he'd never seen in his life before which distracted him, it was incredible how he could even think of following Rosa, let alone doing it. Rosa had to look round often and check on Adam, who was so overwhelmed at the sight and consumed by all the sound that he was almost unable to walk.

Eventually Rosa led him into one of the smaller rooms which contained a few boxes and crates, a table, and a couple of chairs, and sitting on one of them was a red-haired, bearded man who was pulling on the largest pair of boots which Adam had ever seen.

Adam hesitated. He was the outsider. He didn't belong and he knew it...

Chapter Twenty

Adam hesitated, too scared to approach, but Rosa went up to the man at once.

'Sean, here's Adam, the new Kyerna. Adam, this is Sean O'Donnell who will play a Kyerna with you.'

'Erm...Sean, hi,' was all Adam could stutter as Sean looked up from his boots, giving him a grin from behind the beard.

Why am I so shy with strangers? Adam thought.

'Hi there, Adam.'

'Sean,' intercepted Rosa, 'could you help Adam out with the costume please? We need to run a size check, *si*? Let me know when he's done and then we'll check you both together.'

'No trouble at all,' Sean responded jovially. Rosa gave him a smile and left the room.

Adam was fascinated by the boots – they seemed to consume so much of his attention that his head didn't even have enough energy left to look up.

'So Adam,' Sean began, 'I see you like my boots!'

'I...I've never seen any like those before...not ever,' was Adam's hesitant but honest reply. After all the only boots he'd ever worn in the past were football ones. And they were nothing like these – leather, tall, up to just below the knee, with enormous soles and miles of laces.

'Oh, no worries,' Sean replied. 'How long have I been wearin' these for...I've lost count of all the shows I've worn 'em in. I've been doin' this so long that this costume is now part of me!' He grinned again.

There was something in Sean's voice which Adam warmed to – he wasn't the judgemental sort, he wasn't laughing at Adam for never seeing boots like his before – he was encouraging and if at any time Adam needed encouragement, it was then – in that strange situation where he'd never felt so much like an outsider in his life.

Sean stood up with both boots on. 'See? Now when you walk in 'em, you'll find your legs will hurt a bit – mind you, you look strong, have you done anythin' like this before?'

'No, but I play football. I mean – I did play football...'

'That's it then. Strong legs you've got, so wearin' these shouldn't pull your muscles apart too much. But take it slow first, y'know? Get used to 'em. Take your time.'

Sean then strode over to some large boxes, went to a crate and pulled out an identical pair of boots. 'Did Tony get your size?'

'You mean – did I tell him my shoe size? I can't remember.'

'Well, there's only one thing for it then – and that's your tryin' 'em on. But first things first. You need to know which part of this costume's first to put on, then the next piece and so on, see? No use puttin' boots on without the special leggings first!' Sean smiled again, put the boots down and began unloading from one of the boxes.

Adam was speechless as the various costume pieces were laid out before him on the table. Sean arranged them deliberately, so the first pieces were laid out on top, then the next ones to be put on, and so on. The first part was the leggings. Then armour pieces over the knees, followed by the boots.

'Now, it's important the bottom half of the costume be finished first, like. That's because when you've got your top half on you can't bend down very far! You'll be wastin' your time puttin' the boots on last – you won't be able to reach 'em to put 'em on!' Sean's grin became a hearty laugh, and Adam found himself grinning too.

With the leggings on, Adam managed to do the armour up, and then came the boots. 'Good thing you've got them sporty socks on, like,' Sean commented. 'Them towelling ones are great. They'll absorb the sweat – and they'll stay up, too. No embarrassment! I'll tell you somethin' what'll make you laugh. David – the one who usually plays the second Kyerna – once came here without any decent socks on. All he had was the thin things they wear in the office, y'know? Anyway, there he is, in his full costume, boots an' all, and we're halfway through a show and he was having trouble walkin'. Stumblin' around all over the place he was. And those socks had rolled all the way down, right down and round his ankles – and when I helped him take his boots off they were all rolled up on his toes!'

Adam had never known anything like this. There he was, laughing with a total stranger, while holding in his hands the largest pair of boots he'd ever seen. It was many years since he last felt this happy. Even being on the winning team at the football game was nothing in comparison to this. Football was great to be part of, to play in the team and to do well – and to hear the sound of the crowd when the team won – but it was nothing like this. Maybe it was just being with Sean, the person rather than the situation; while Sean was talking to him, Adam felt very much aware that if someone like Sean would have been the team captain a couple of evenings prior, that dreadful incident after his last match would never have happened.

Adam was fortunate to find that the boots fitted – it took him a while to get used to the weight, and the lack of movement, but soon Sean was teaching him a way of walking which both complimented the character while helping him at the same time. After the boots were on, there was a thin, tight black garment on the upper body, upon which several pieces of what looked like steel armour were positioned. Adam donned a neck seal, which felt very strange around the neck, almost like he had his neck in a sling, followed by more armour over the top. Then followed the dark crimson robes Adam had seen on the photo before in Hewitt's office.

'It's important now that you get used to wearin' that helmet, see, while you're in full costume and before the rehearsal starts,' Sean advised. 'Try puttin' it on now, before the gloves go on, see? It's very tough when the gloves are on.'

This was the bit Adam had been looking forward to the most. To be able to wear that helmet which he could disappear into – to take another role other than his own – to be able to hide all his emotions away from the world and its prying eyes! As Sean handed the helmet to him, Adam felt an enormous surge of emotion which caused a small tremble. Sean interpreted this as fear.

'No worries, you won't break it! Take your time, hold it tight. I think you should stand in front of that mirror over there, so you can put it on properly.'

Sean was pointing to a full-length mirror on the opposite wall – and Adam gazed in sheer wonder, amazed at the transformation. Seeing himself in costume for the first time, helmet in

hand, another shiver of emotion ran through him.
Thinking that the helmet would be much safer on
his head than in his hands, he raised it up. Sean
went over to help him – and just a couple of
minutes later there he was, in full costume except
for gloves, hidden, disappeared, and he was free
to express any emotion he wished with no
interference from the world whatsoever. Nobody
could see him. Nobody could tell it was him.
The feeling was overwhelming.

'Now try a few steps,' Sean prompted.
'You see me ok? Now, walk towards me the way
I showed you.'

Adam took his first tentative steps
forward; Sean stopped him, and then taught him
to turn left and right.

'Now you're doing good. Take that
helmet off for a while. How's that feel?'

'Er...incredible,' Adam replied, his hot,
red face appearing from beneath the helmet. 'Just
incredible.'

'Now, I'm going to get ready. I'm half-
done and won't take long. I'm used to this! How
far can you walk in the boots?

'I think I can walk better now.'

'Do you think you can do me a favour? Go and find Rosa, get her here and then we can run that sizin' check. But take your time now, there'll be stuff all over those corridors and we can't afford to have you trippin' up!'

Adam gave Sean a grin and then set off. Sean was right. The corridors were piled high with crates and boxes. The weapons Adam saw earlier had all been taken into the main hall but there were packets, bubble wrap and bags scattered all around where they had been. He was careful not to tread on any of them – he had no idea just how those boots would react to having something slippery to walk on.

'Rosa?' he called out just outside the main hall.

'What is it?' came a reply.

'It's Adam here. Sean sent me to find you. He's just finishing putting his costume on now, and he says it's time for the sizing check.'

'Right.' Rosa came out into the corridor, dressed in a combination of various types of leather, bone and armour. She was amazed when she saw Adam. '*Bene! Ottimo*! You look fantastic!'

'Thanks very much.' Adam found himself having problems accepting compliments. He just looked back at her.

Rosa interpreted his behaviour as stress. 'You feel OK? Not too tired or too hot?'

'I'm fine,' Adam slowly dragged himself back to normal. 'It's a good thing I had something to eat before I came out here. Dr Hewitt – er...Tony – he told me to have something to eat. I can see why!'

'Come on then,' Rosa said, leading the way down. 'Getting used to the boots?'

'Just about! I was telling Sean, I've never ever seen any boots like these before.'

'Slow down,' Rosa replied, pointing to a very unstable pile of crates which looked like it would tip over any second. 'Stay towards the wall, keep behind me.'

By the time they reached Sean, he was nearly fully ready. They waited until his helmet was on, then Adam put on his own helmet and Rosa sized them up together. There was just a small difference in the height, which Rosa corrected by helping Sean remove one of the lifts in his boots. It was the easiest option, since the alternative would to have been to get Adam put lifts in his, which would be impractical for a new person to have to go through. It was not an easy procedure to alter the boots with Sean in full costume, and Rosa dealt with one of the boots while another group member called Joseph did the other.

'It's your fault, Adam!' Sean laughed.

Adam was startled. 'What do you mean?'

'I have to take both these damn boots off just for you. I hope you appreciate that! Why can't you be as tall as Dave?'

Adam looked round, taken aback at first, but was reassured when he saw all three of them smiling.

'You've not been teased yet, Adam, have you?' asked Joseph. 'You'll have to get used to that if you perform with us!'

'Come on everyone, let's all practice!' said Rosa excitedly.

Chapter Twenty-one

I'm in costume.

I've a helmet on, a crimson cape, armour, padding and heavy black boots.

Nobody knows who I am or what I'm thinking. Nobody knows how I'm feeling. I've disappeared.

I'm not myself any more. I'm someone else. I'm the true me, the person I have to hide from the world every day to survive in it.

I know where I need to stand and what I need to do.

I've a large mace in my hand, a special one which glows with power. It's called an 'Alkar.' I'm standing here, with my fellow Kyerna, fellow Dark Protector, poised ready for combat beside our master, the Kyrah, Gandoren.

The battle begins. First the Kosan warriors approach us, blades drawn, shields up, and led by Liapi. Then come the Zenar combat soldiers, the Kosan chiefs, and large battle droids. Gandoren stands, leading his troopers into battle, and we follow behind.

One of the Kosan chiefs comes for me. I pose aggressively but he's not intimidated, so with one glow of my Alkar he's down. A shield of troopers surrounds me, but they are soon cut down by the Kosan warriors.

I'm then left alone facing one of the Zenar combat soldiers. He approaches by the right, I attack first to his left then make a sharp turn, catching him from the rear on his right, which he is unprepared for. I watch him fall, and then raise my Alkar high as a signal for the next wave of troopers to enter the battle.

Gandoren then calls. I hear him shout...

'Adam?'

'W...what?'

'You are falling asleep?'

'Er...no, no, just thinking...' He looked up slowly, trying to bring himself back into reality.

Rosa's smiling face was looking down at him.

'Sorry.'

'No need for sorry, Adam! You were brilliant. *Ottimo*!'

'*Ottimo*?'

'In Italia, how we say it's excellent.'

Adam slowly smiled back. 'Well, in that case then, I'd certainly say it was '*Ottimo*' – I've never enjoyed something so much, it wasn't just what we were doing, it was the people too...'

'Well, tomorrow we have now; we do it all over again, *si*? Just like today. Only tomorrow we'll have the crowds watching us!'

'You were amazing, and I want to thank you all for letting me do this. Where's...er...Tony?'

'He's just giving the troopers a hand with their uniforms, taking them off. We all help each other.'

Adam felt a tinge of guilt. 'Oh no! I've just been dreaming here and there's work to be done...I'm sorry...' He tried to get up but, still being half-dressed in costume, and with boots on, he couldn't do it.

'That's no trouble. Everyone new does this. They all tire quickly, they aren't used to it. Now, let me get those boots off. '

Hewitt entered the room. Because Adam was used to his lecturer's face white with anger, he didn't recognise the red, sweaty face as he entered.

'Adam! Well done, that was amazing.'

'Ah, Tony!' interposed Rosa, looking up from the boots. 'Adam was asking about you.'

'Er...Tony?' Adam still had trouble calling him by his first name. 'Sorry...I wanted to thank you for inviting me here. And – and for making me a part of this group.'

'I take it then that you enjoyed it?'

'I've never known anything like this,' Adam replied.

Tony smiled back.

'I just wish I could do it all the time. No, please don't get me wrong,' Adam corrected himself quickly, 'I'm very grateful for you allowing me into this group, and for giving me this chance tomorrow, and for meeting so many people. But after tomorrow...well...next week, everything will be different...'

'Come on, finish getting changed,' Tony interrupted suddenly. He looked at Rosa, who had finished stacking the boots, and continued – 'Rosa, can you do something for me? We all need to meet together in a few minutes and discuss what time we all need to be here tomorrow. Try and see if everyone can be here by eleven, so we can be all ready to perform at one.'

As soon as Rosa left the room, Hewitt closed the door.

'Now Adam, listen,' he began in a low voice, 'I'm the only one here who knows about what you're doing at that university. They all told me what was going to happen and what to expect, even before you did it. I'm your lecturer; I had the right to know. I know all about it – and also about next week, how you're due to go back in that machine and return to the person you were previously.'

Adam was shocked. 'You know about the experiment? Everything?'

'I had to,' Hewitt replied sharply. 'It was my job to know. It was important. It took me ages to get all the information. Now I know what I need to do. I've a question for you.'

Adam stared back blankly, frightened of what Hewitt could say next.

'I want to know – well, I want to know how you feel about going back to how you were. How do you feel about going back to be your real self, the real Adam?'

'I'm torn,' was the sad reply as Adam looked down at the floor. 'I want to play in goal again, with Brad as my best mate instead of my worst enemy. But I also want to be here, to be in this group. I know that without that experiment I would never have met Sean, or Rosa, or Joseph...and tomorrow would have been a normal Saturday, but instead we will be performing.'

'Do you know about your work, your degree? How this experiment has changed your work?'

'Yes,' Adam nodded. 'I can do it; all of a sudden I can do it.'

'Can I ask another question? Be as honest as you can.'

'OK.'

148

'If you had a choice would you return? If the choice was yours, no department decisions, nothing – would you go back, or not?'

'But it is the department decision!' Adam blurted out. 'That's it. Monday, that's the lot. That afternoon I'll be going back...back to be the person – the person...'

'Yes?'

'No.'

'Come again?'

'No!' Adam repeated with emphasis. 'That person who I was, you say that's my real self, but it isn't! Not now! How can it be? I'm not the same...I'm not that person any more. I've...well...changed somehow...'

'And now we have your answer.'

'But – the department...'

'Never mind that department!' Hewitt snapped back angrily. 'I'll be in there doing my best to make sure it doesn't happen! Monday morning, I'm free and I know you've a study period. Everyone will be in that engineering room setting up. I'm going to confront them. I want you there with me. Together, we'll do our damnedest to make sure you won't go back, that you'll never go back!'

The door opened and Rosa's head appeared. 'Is everything alright? I heard raised voices...'

'Everything's fine.' Hewitt turned, automatically replying with an artificial smile. 'I'm still in "anger mode" after that rehearsal!'

'Save it till tomorrow!' smiled Rosa. 'You'll need it!'

'Can everyone get here tomorrow by eleven?'

'I think so.'

'Right. Come on Adam, let's get you finished and then we'll all meet up and arrange tomorrow's transport. The hall's available overnight so we can store all our stuff here. And Adam,' he said, in a lower tone, 'don't worry about anything. I mean, anything.'

Adam smiled back.

Chapter Twenty-two

Adam was emotional.

The crowds were coming through the doors, so he was feeling stressed. He was worried for fear that he'd stand in the wrong place, at the wrong time, and though in the past he'd seen lots of crowds at his football games, he wasn't used to them being so close to him. If anything went wrong, that crowd would know in seconds. *I must get it right,* he told himself again and again.

'Adam, are you ready?' came a familiar voice.

'Yes, Rosa,' he replied hesitantly.

'No worries, no? Excellent. Do you remember how we say it's excellent?'

'*Ottimo.*'

'That's right! And if you can remember that, you'll remember everything else we said and did last night!' She laughed.

Adam smiled faintly.

Rosa reached out a hand. 'You'll be fine! Look, I'll finish helping you with your costume, and then we'll organise the starting positions. How's that?'

'You've been so kind to me,' was the only thing Adam could think of to say in reply.

'You've been kind to us. With David ill, we needed another Kyerna, and here you are.'

'I know I won't be as good as David.'

'All you need to remember is this. You take the battle at the point where the first Kosan chief approaches you. Now, when you pose to threaten him, you think of your worst enemy. Have you got one, someone who really dislikes you?'

Adam instantly thought of Brad. 'Yes, I have someone in mind.'

'Good, now I want you to think of him while you're posing. Let that anger come out, then everyone will be able to see it through that costume!'

All too easy, thought Adam, knowing that all it took was one thought about his ex-best mate and his temper would naturally go through the roof.

Rosa kept talking to him, reminding him about his part and prompting him as his costume was being put on. By the time the helmet was on, Adam was much more confident about the performance, and when Tony stuck his head round the door to tell everyone it was time to take their starting positions, Adam was actually looking forward to it. They all went out to a storm of applause – Adam was thankful he had the helmet, since it muffled some of the sound – and they all arranged themselves exactly as they had done when they had rehearsed the night before.

Adam was in his element. It all came naturally to him, the emotion flowing through him. He concentrated on his role. There were no crowds anymore, no sea of eyes watching him, no people recognising him, nobody waiting to tease him. He was one of the Kyerna, protecting his master; he was a Dark Protector, fighting by the side of Gandoren; he had troops to command, a battle to fight, a war to win and a part to play, and his whole mind was concentrating fully on it. It was like he was part of a dream, yet in a sense this dream was real; he was in the real world, yet

153

not part of it; his body was living in one world, while his mind and heart were in another.

He had remembered what Rosa had suggested; he saw Brad clear as crystal, and the anger flooded through him, out of the costume and into the waiting crowd, who felt it in a wave. They reacted, some backing away slightly, sensing the power behind the pose.

The performance went on - the crowd were astounded; children were shouting and screaming, cameras and phones were snapping shots and recording; yet to Adam none of this was happening. From the first positions as the battle started, down to the last scene as Gandoren squared up to Liapi, Adam, had only a faint perception of the actual world – it was as if that helmet was preventing him from seeing it all in more ways than one.

He could feel the final round of applause beneath his feet. The clapping vibrated through those thick soles, the shouts and whoops were penetrating through those layers of metal and leather. As the group took its final step forward towards the crowd, Adam felt his face was wet with sweat and tears.

Who am I?

He felt sadness all of a sudden hitting him hard. Soon he'd be out of character. It was all over. It was back to the changing room. Then the next day off to recover, where he'd be doing nothing but lounging about all day. Then it would be Monday. Monday - the day when all this would be over, never to return. He'd certainly be out of character then – out of character in reality.

Standing there, in front of the crowds for the last final pose, he felt the dreadful feeling of absolute finality – as if the world was really going to end, and he had no power to stop it.

He limped his way back to the changing areas. Rosa was alongside him, telling him how wonderful his performance was but he hardly heard it.

Soon it would be Monday.

Chapter Twenty-three

After a rather dull, miserable Sunday full of worry, Adam stumbled his way back through the university corridors on Monday morning. Hewitt had arranged a meeting in his office first at ten, and he was there on time – in a highly emotional state, but there on time.

Hewitt was waiting. He was holding Adam's essay in his hand.

'You see this?' he began.

'Yes.'

'Aside from all the other issues, this is the main reason why I want to do everything I can to stop you going back this afternoon. This is your essay. Remember it?'

'Only just,' Adam replied hesitantly. To him, that essay was written a very long time ago.

'It was only last Tuesday when you wrote it, surely you remember? I was at the library – do you remember seeing me there? And the seminar I gave the following day?'

'Yes, I can remember that now,' Adam answered, grateful for the prompts he was given to help him recollect the events of such a traumatic week.

'Well, I invited you here on Thursday morning to talk about this essay. But when you arrived, you were overcome with what happened at that football game, then you were talking about that helmet...well, it all went on from there and I never had time to talk about it properly to you.'

Adam paused, expecting another temper, but his lecturer was smiling.

'Have a look at the mark I've given you for this.'

Adam stared, making no move.

'Come on, take it!'

Adam obeyed, more out of fear than curiosity. He wanted to avoid trouble more than anything else in the world. When he took the paper with trembling hands, he looked at the mark on it. He stared at Hewitt, blinked, and looked again.

'I don't believe it.'

'You don't believe this, or me?'

'I don't understand – I only had a day to do this, remember, the library – it just seemed so natural, so real. I'd no idea you'd like it so much.'

'I gave that essay the highest mark that's been given out to a first-year since the course was started. Why did I do that, if I didn't like it?'

Adam stared back, totally puzzled. 'I don't know. It must have been a – a one-off, that's all.'

'A one-off?' Evidence for his final decision was mounting at speed now.

'Yeah,' Adam replied, with emphasis. 'A one-off. That's all it is. It's just one of those things that happen. You know, when things just happen, without thinking? It's just that for the first time in my life I seemed to know what I was doing and I could understand what it was you needed from me. I didn't need to ask any more. I didn't need to put it off any more. I knew what to do, I went ahead and did it, and that's it. Here it is. But I don't know if I could do it again. So to me it's a one-off and that's all it is.'

'What if I was to make sure there would be other essays like this, not one-offs but real essays with more marks like this one?'

'I'd be happy. I shouldn't tell you this really but I used to get Amy to help me out all the time. I don't want her to get into trouble for helping me but I'd have never made it this far without her help. She used to help me with the work. To me it wasn't important, I was always late and if it wasn't for her I'd never have got anything done on time.'

Hewitt was determined. 'The final decision's your own but I don't want you to go back. If you do, you'll be losing out on a good degree. You'll be asking Amy to help you again. But that decision is your own.'

'I'm supposed to be there in an hour to do the final video with Liz and Ed...'

'And you will be,' Hewitt replied. 'There's nothing wrong with the experiment in itself. I'm all for getting more people into this university who have the potential to learn, and seeing what support is needed for them to be their best. The results are important and that's what that video is for. But what I'm against is you returning, going back.'

'But...but...' stuttered Adam.'

'But what?'

'If I go back and do that video, the next thing they'll do is take me straight over to that machine and put me in it! Then I've got to go back, I've got to return and nothing can stop it...

Hewitt nodded.

Chapter Twenty-four

Liz looked up brightly from her monitor as Adam came through the door.

'Everything's all set, Adam!'

'Ready?' Ed said, coming over with his coat pockets full of tools, as usual. 'Remember what your last job was?'

'To do the video on here,' Adam replied, 'then after it's done, I'm to go to the cafe and get a drink with sugar in it.'

'Right!' smiled Ed. 'Dr Keller will need to be monitoring your blood sugar levels and it's so important that they don't crash through the floor!'

'We've got some great information from this experiment about special needs,' Dinesh said, coming over. 'There have been some amazing things happening. What's that badge you're wearing?'

'Er...this one? It's a VGP logo – the Vorna Galaxy Players. We were performing at the local comic con last Saturday and all wear a badge like this - they get it on their first performance.'

'Now you can tell us all about it,' Liz replied, loading the final video file up for Adam, who sat down and took the mic for the last time.

'Well...here I am again and after the best weekend I've ever had, thanks to Tony...er..sorry, Dr Hewitt, and his amazing group, Rosa, Sean, Joseph and the others. I was proud to do this for them after David Atkins got ill and they needed a replacement. It was amazing, the crowd, everyone, I can't believe it's all over.'

'How do you feel now this experiment is finishing?' Liz asked.

'A bit sad,' Adam replied. 'I don't think things will be the same. Liz – when I'm back, will I remember all this?'

'Of course you will, just like you can remember now the way it was before this experiment started.'

'You remember me?' Dinesh prompted, 'I've known you longer than anyone else here, remember us at school?'

Adam paused, remembering. 'I'll never forget when I laughed at you when you said you wanted to be a scientist! But...now, I can't understand why I laughed at you. To me you're a scientist and you always were.'

'Adam,' Liz cut in, 'Tell us about what's going to happen after this recording finishes.'

'I've got to go to the cafe first, because I need a drink high in sugar before I go back.'

'Shall I go and pick one up for him while he's doing this?' Dinesh asked. 'It'll save time.'

'That's a good idea,' Ed began, but Adam cut in.

'No – no, I'll do it, I – I need some fresh air,' he replied hastily.

'OK, no problem,' Ed smiled as Adam breathed a sigh of relief.

'Anything else to say on the video?' asked Liz.

'Just the fact that I'm certainly going to miss the Vorna Galaxy Players, and I'll have to work about ten times as hard on that degree too. But at least I'll be back on the team, back playing football. I haven't got a clue what's been happening because Brad's not speaking to me anymore.'

'I'm sure things are as they've always been with the team, and when you go back you'll be playing again. It'll be just how it was before. Things will be the same.'

'No, they won't be, Liz!'

'Dinesh, what do you mean?'

'What's going on with that football team, it won't be the same. Brad's gone. One of the guys owned up to the coach last weekend about that incident on Wednesday and it was worse than you told us. You told everyone you were booted out for dropping the ball when in goal but what you never said was how Brad reacted after that match. When the coach heard about it, he was furious and dropped Brad from the team.'

Rather than being pleased, Adam was terrified. 'But – that means Brad'll blame me for all this and he'll be after me!'

'No way, we won't let that happen,' Dinesh reassured him. 'If he goes anywhere near you he'll be out this university. You know who'll be keeping an eye on him?'

'You?'

'Me! And Amy of course, since she does the same degree as you both so can keep an eye on things. But Brad's not even after you. He's too busy trying to find the member of his team who owned up and dropped him in it, so he won't be bothering about you.'

Adam wasn't convinced. He sat sadly at the mic, not speaking.

'Go out for your drink now, Adam,' Liz said encouragingly.

Adam sighed. 'Oh well. May as well, won't be long.' He picked his rucksack up. 'Anyone else here want a drink?'

'No we're all fine,' Liz replied. Adam left the room, listening to Liz's instructions as he closed the door slowly behind him.

'Ed, start the initiation sequence. Joe, run the final computer checks. Machine check, everything must be on go by the time Adam gets back. Dinesh, call Dr Keller and tell him to be here in half an hour, and tell him not to forget the rehydration kit. Adam might need it. Glass of water, somebody, over here just in case.'

But before Dinesh could get to the telephone, it started ringing.

'Engineering department?'

Someone spoke sharply at the other end. Dinesh looked round.

'Er...Liz, it's for you.'

'What?'

'It's for you...I don't know who it is but he says it's important.'

Chapter Twenty-five

Adam managed to stumble into the cafe, grab the most sugar-laden coffee he could get and drag himself back to the department, drinking it slowly along the way. But he heard the raised voices long before he reached the building. He stopped outside in the grounds, not daring to enter.

Just then Dinesh came out. 'Adam!'

'What's going on?'

'I don't know. Liz and Ed are having a row with some lecturer. He was told to leave but he wouldn't, so Liz dismissed everyone for half an hour and that included me. I tried hanging around to see what I could pick up but I can't tell what they're saying.'

'Which lecturer?'

'A tall guy with a white face and a very bad temper.'

'That'll be Hewitt!'

'Who?'

'Dr Hewitt, you remember. He teaches most of my modules, he said he was going to do something, something to stop it...'

'Stop what?'

'The experiment!'

'But he can't stop it. Nobody can. Everything's all been set up; it's been all agreed...'

'I know that, but he doesn't! He'll do anything on earth to...'

'But why does he want to stop it in the first place?'

'Come on, I'll tell you. I can't hear a thing with that argument going on. Let's find somewhere quiet. It's too noisy round here.'

Inside there was a heated debate going on. Liz and Ed now sat at a table, opposite an enraged Dr Hewitt.

'Absolutely not. I couldn't possibly! The very idea is absurd!'

'I agree with Liz. What you're saying, Tony, is against the regulations of the contract

Adam signed, as well as our ethical principles here at this university.'

'But don't you realise what this means?' Hewitt stormed. 'Adam has potential – the most potential I've ever seen in fifteen years of teaching this module! And I won't let this talent be sacrificed for the sake of the results of an experiment!'

Liz leaned forward. 'But, even without stating contracts – the person who's the real Adam isn't the person who you're teaching! Adam won't be himself until he comes back to his natural state. Adam is the person he was before – the person you knew before; he's the person we all knew. He's not himself...'

'He's himself now!' Hewitt argued. 'Can't you see what's happened? He's really learning, for the first time in his life! What on earth gives you the right to take this from him? He has the opportunity for a future – a decent career – you will be taking this away from him and I will do my damnedest not to let you!'

Ed did his best to try and diffuse the situation and calm Hewitt down. 'Tony,' he began gently, 'I don't think you realise how much he's suffered with all this. He's been thrown off the football team, which he used to love. That was a big part of his life, you know it was. And he's also lost his best friend. Another of his friends hardly recognises him anymore, poor Amy, and she's afraid for him. Is that the life you want for him, Tony? Think about that!'

Hewitt leaned towards Ted. 'Fine. I'll think about it. But you think about this! I teach him! I know him far better than you do! And I know talent when I see it. I've taught this module for fifteen years. I can see the future head of my department right here, here in the making – in front of my eyes – and no way in hell will I – '

There was a knock at the door.

'Come in!'

Adam entered first. He was accompanied by Dinesh and Amy.

Dinesh spoke first. 'It's only us. Sorry for interrupting, but we were outside and wanted to know what was going on, and because it's something to do with Adam we think he should be here to hear it.'

There was a pause. Adam struggled to get the confidence to speak.

'I know what you're arguing about. It's me, isn't it?'

'We're not arguing,' began Liz. 'We're just having a debate.'

'It's about me though, isn't it?'

'Yes it is!' Hewitt broke in. 'I'm trying to get people to see some sense here and recognise potential when they see it!'

'Calm down, Tony,' Ed replied, offering Adam a seat. 'Adam, here's what's going on. Come and sit down.'

Adam, conscious of everyone's eyes on him, slowly took a chair. He felt sick.

'Can - can we stay?' Amy began. 'I'm worried about Adam.'

'Of course you can,' Ed replied.

'Thank you,' Dinesh said, also sitting down and inviting Amy to the seat next to him.

Ed, looking at Adam's pale face, decided there was no point in delaying any longer. 'Adam, it's like this. Over the last few days, we've all seen changes in you, that's the point of our experiment, that's what it was for, and today you are expected to return to the person you were before. But Dr Hewitt here has been telling us all about your essay and the improvements he's seen in you, and he says he doesn't want you to return to the person you were in the past.'

'I certainly don't!' Hewitt interrupted sharply.

Ed gave him a quick look, and then continued.

'However, Liz and I feel that you must go back, since we believe that the person you used to be is the person you really are. All you are now is the result of the experiment, we don't even know if these effects you're experiencing now are permanent! It was only supposed to be for a week, that's all it was ever meant to be for. It wasn't designed to change a person forever. Anything could happen...'

'But does all this mean I have a choice? I mean, can I choose whether or not to go back?'

'Well, I'm not sure...' began Liz.

'Why shouldn't Adam have a choice?' Amy asked. 'He volunteered for this! He stuck his neck out for this! He lost his place in the football team because of this. Surely he has the right to choose!'

'Dinesh, what do you think?' asked Ed. 'You're the one who selected him for this experiment, and you've known him the longest.'

'Well,' Dinesh started, trying to collect both his thoughts and the hard facts of the experiment together all at once, 'there's no doubt Adam's been an excellent candidate for this experiment. We have some great results, which will no doubt be used to help provide support for many students one day. But I see the experiment as one issue and Adam as another. It's not about an experiment; it's about a human being. Now, to me it doesn't matter about experiments any more. If Adam is coherent and intelligent enough to make a decision, which we know he is' - here Hewitt nodded assent – 'then does it matter who he is? If, say, you invented a machine which turned a white person into someone who was black, do you think as a black person he'd have less right to choose things for himself? Of course not! To me, it's the same in this case. You must agree with that, Ed, as a black person!'

Ed smiled. 'I know what you mean.'

'That is the way I see it anyway,' Dinesh concluded, 'It's about a human and not an experiment anymore. I'm here to study science and as a scientist I can see there's a difference between an experiment and a person.'

Hewitt nodded vigorously.

Liz looked directly at Adam, and spoke gently to him. Adam, upset from the stress around him, could hardly hold up his head; but Liz knew he was able to both hear her and understand her, and had the intelligence to respond.

'Adam, Amy's right, you were the volunteer, and you were the guinea pig. But your time is almost up. It's my wish, and Ed's too I believe, that this afternoon you return to the person you were before this experiment started. However, your lecturer here doesn't see it that way. He feels now that you must stay as you are, since he can see a career ahead for you and a future. But know this, Adam' – she paused as Adam looked up – 'that if you decide to stay, stay as you are now, then that will be your choice. However, the equipment must be dismantled at the end of today. That's according to the terms and conditions of the equipment manufacturers and other stakeholders, that everything be dismantled and finished by tonight. Do you know why that's so important?'

'I'm not sure...' Adam's head was swimming.

'It's because we can't take the risk of someone else using all this for the wrong purpose, or use it without knowledge. It could make someone seriously ill. This equipment is dangerous if people don't know how to use it properly. We must take everything in here to pieces and clear these rooms by midnight tonight.'

'You know what that means for you?' Ed said. 'It means if you decide not to go back, you'll never ever be going back.'

'Big decision,' agreed Liz.

Dinesh looked over at Adam, as did Amy. Liz and Ed were now silent. Even Hewitt was waiting, not interrupting.

Adam slowly got up, and then silently walked over to the huge glass chamber. He smiled, got into it, and lay down.

Chapter Twenty-six

Two weeks had now elapsed since the experiment had taken place, but the university had not changed, neither had the weather. Students continued to provide the only colour among the grey buildings. Lunch breaks had not changed, with the perpetual noise and chatter over sandwiches and coffee.

Dinesh hadn't changed either. He was still taking coffee in the cafe, clad in his bright white lab coat, Amy and Adam with him. 'What are you doing tomorrow, Adam?'

'I've got a rehearsal with the players. They're amazing. Sean keeps on and on wanting us to go to Dublin!'

'Looks like you'll be travelling then!'

'Ireland's nothing in comparison to what Rosa wants. I've lost count of how many times she wants us to go to Italy.' He looked down at the table.

'You seem a bit upset?'

'I'm a bit afraid of going somewhere where I don't speak the language.'

'Remember you can learn, if you get the support,' Dinesh encouraged.

'Even a foreign language?'

'Yes, even a foreign language.'

'I'd love to learn Italian.'

'There'll be no time for football practice if you did,' Dinesh grinned.

'I'm trying to practice all I can. The new captain's trying me in defence. It's very hard work but he says there's a chance if I practice hard. I'm determined.'

'Have you finished your essay for Dr Hewitt yet?' Dinesh asked.

'He's already had it,' was the instant reply.

'What, already?'

'Yes,' Adam was emphatic. 'I finished it a week ago and gave it to him after his lecture.'

'Tell Dinesh what he said when you gave it to him!' interjected Amy.

'Oh, do I have to?'

'Yes you do! Don't be shy!'

Adam paused and lowered his head before replying. Amy gave his elbow a small push.

'Well...Dr Hewitt said he'd never known a student to be able to write it in a short time. We're going through it during tutorial and...'

He paused.

'Go on!'

'Um...well, he said if this one was as good as the other one, then there's a good chance I'd be getting a first at this degree.'

Dinesh was thrilled. 'That's brilliant. Well done!'

Adam looked back, showing no emotion. 'I suppose so.'

Dinesh started laughing. Amy soon followed, and Adam slowly broke into a smile.

1114586OR00109

Printed in Great Britain
by Amazon